Shandra Higl

Double Duplicity

Tarnished Remains

Deadly Aim

Murderous Secrets

Murderous Secrets
A Shandra Higheagle Mystery

Paty Jager

Windtree Press

MURDEROUS SECRETS
Copyright © 2015 Patricia Jager

Contact Information: info@windtreepress.com

Windtree Press
4660 NE Belknap Court
Suite 101-O
Hillsboro, OR 97124
Visit us at http://windtreepress.com

Cover Art by Christina Keerins

Published in the United States of America
ISBN 9781943601394

Dedication

Special thanks to Carmen Peone for giving me a tour of the Colville Reservation and insights into the people who live there.

Chapter One

Shandra Higheagle sat up in bed. Her heart raced and her mind replayed the dream in vivid detail.

Ella, Grandmother, *stood in the middle of stampeding horses. Her long bony finger pointed at a mangled body on the ground. Shandra wanted to turn her eyes from the sight, but the hat with the beaded hat band on the ground next to the mangled body brought a feeling of safety and love that eased her lonely soul. The wind shrieked. Shandra's gaze flashed to her grandmother. Tears trickled down Ella's cheeks. The horses stopped and all circled the body, their muzzles pointed inward to...her father.*

Shandra scrubbed her face with her hands. She'd had this same dream every night for the last week. Finding the truth behind her father's death was the only way she'd ever have a good night's sleep and relieve her mind.

The red glowing numbers on the clock beside the bed told her she might as well get up. A couple more hours and Aunt Jo would be awake. She'd call, giving her aunt warning of Shandra's arrival that afternoon. There was no sense in putting the trip to the reservation off any longer. Her mother and stepfather wouldn't give her any information about her father's death, but the Higheagle family, hopefully, would fill her in on the details she needed to know.

Sheba, her large, slobbery, mutt of several large breed dogs, raised her basketball-sized head and stared at her.

"I know, you don't like to get up this early. I have things to finish in the studio if I'm going to the reservation today." Shandra slipped her feet into fuzzy slippers and wandered out of her bedroom. A deep sigh and thud in the room behind her tipped her lips into a smile. Sheba might not like to get up this early, but she won't allow me out of her sight.

Shandra continued through the great room, glancing at the laptop she'd left open on the heavy, wood coffee table. She'd run into dead ends while trying to search online for records of her father's death.

On the way to the kitchen, her gaze landed on a photo of her father on the bookcase. He was holding up a large belt buckle and grinning. Her heart stirred, remembering those same hands holding her and whispering in her ear that life was a mystery and to live uncovering every clue. She'd only been four when her father died, but she remembered nearly every moment they'd spent together that year.

She walked over and held up the photograph and ran a finger over her father's face. Memory was a funny thing. More and more of her fourth year on this earth came back to her as she dug to discover if her father's death was an accident or intentional. She remembered traveling to the rodeos as a family, but then tagging along with her father because mom disappeared. Almost as if she didn't want to be seen with her Native American husband and half-breed daughter.

She shook her head. "That couldn't be. Could it?"

Sheba pushed against Shandra's thigh with her head.

"I know, if you're up, you're hungry." She ruffled the black fur on Sheba's head and continued to the kitchen.

Shandra started the tea kettle, poured kibble into Sheba's bowl, and refreshed her water. The kettle whistled. Plucking one of her own mugs from the open-front cupboard, Shandra poured steaming water into the cup and dropped in a tea ball with green tea leaves.

While the tea steeped, she debated when to call Ryan. While his office was all of Weippe County, his county detective work kept him stationed in and around the county seat of Warner. But if he happened to be in the area and stopped by, he'd get worried if she wasn't home. Unlike her mother, who wasn't so much worried about her daughter but about what rumors may get started by Shandra's exploits, Detective Ryan Greer did genuinely care what happened to her. A smile started at her lips and infused joy in her heart. They'd only been dating three months, but she had a closer connection to him than any man in her life up to now.

Thinking of her last disastrous relationship, her brow scrunched and the joy seeped from her chest. If she'd been older, more worldly, she would have made that sadistic professor pay for the way he'd treated her.

Sheba woofed at the door, dissipating her anger. Shandra pulled on a coat, shoved her feet into fuzzy boots, opened the door, picked up her tea, and headed down the path carved in the eighteen inches of snow to the studio.

The moon still clung to the dark sky spattered with stars. A blush of pink flirted in the eastern sky. This time of morning held a special appeal for Shandra. The bright stars slowly fading as the sun crept over the horizon. The cold snow sparkled like diamonds and squeaked under her feet.

The promise of another day.

She stopped a moment to savor her life on the mountain. This ranch she'd purchased nearly three years ago had captured her heart from the first moment she set foot on the land. Finding the clay deposits she needed for her vases added to the feeling she'd found her home.

Sheba bounded out of the pine trees behind the house, studio, and barn. She skidded to a stop at the door to the studio.

Shandra laughed at the big dog's puppy-like antics and continued to the studio. She opened the door, and Sheba lay down in her usual spot under the glazing table. As she grew, Sheba had learned to stay under the table to avoid being told to move every five minutes.

Shandra flicked on the bright overhead lights and headed to the kiln. The drying unit was filled with the small coasters she made as souvenirs for the local businesses to sell. They were mindless squares of clay she etched Huckleberry Mountain on and glazed. Lil, her employee and a stray that came with the property, had learned how to make the clay squares, freeing up more of Shandra's time to work on her high-end vases.

That was why she needed to get this load of coasters out of the kiln. She needed to start a slow glazing process she was perfecting on a vase she planned to reveal at a February art show in New Mexico.

"What are you doing up?" Lil's voice crackled in the silent building.

Shandra spun around. Her fingers opened and several kiln-dried coasters sailed through the air.

"You don't have to throw things at me." Lil said, picking the shattered pieces up off the floor.

"You startled me. I thought Sheba and I were the only ones awake." Shandra held back the grin twitching her lips. Lil had on a wild, purple flowered shirt under her usual, purple wool coat that she wore in the winter. Faded purple corduroy pants that had many ribs worn off covered the older woman's legs. Lil's short white hair stuck out in tufts under the lavender stocking cap on her head. Like a mink collar on the coat, a large orange cat hung around Lil's neck. Both Lewis, the cat, and Lil came with the property.

The ranch had been in Lil's family for two generations. But when the grandparents who raised her started having health issues, the ranch was sold to pay their doctor bills. There had been two owners between Lil's grandparents and Shandra. Both had kicked Lil off the property when she tried to squat on the land. Shandra saw Lil's skills and offered her a job. The eccentric woman made a room for herself and Lewis in the tack room in the barn.

"At this hour, it's usually only Lewis and I that are awake." Lil set the cat down on a chair and walked over to the kiln.

"I had a dream that woke me. I've decided to visit my aunt today and wanted to get that newly glazed vase in the kiln." Shandra avoided making eye contact with Lil. The woman knew a bit about Shandra's grandmother coming to her in dreams, but Ryan was the only person she'd told everything about her dreams. She'd had to or end up in jail for a murder she didn't commit.

"Why this sudden trip to see your aunt?" Lil picked up several coasters and carried them over to the table housing Sheba.

"It's not sudden. I've been thinking about it for a month." Ever since she'd revisited Phil Seeton, a cowboy that had rodeoed with her father, and he'd suggested Edward Higheagle's rodeo accident wasn't an accident.

"You never brought it up."

The accusing tone in Lil's voice drew Shandra's attention. She watched the older woman walk back to the kiln and reach into the depths. The large round ceramic oven appearing to swallow the woman up to her waist.

"That's because I wasn't positive I needed to go. I am now." She waited her turn to grab more of the coasters.

Lil straightened from the kiln and peered into her eyes. "Detective Greer know you're going?"

Her reference to Ryan as detective was typical Lil. Since Ryan had thought Lil had killed her fiancé thirty years ago, Lil hadn't been too friendly with him. But she didn't say anything about Shandra seeing him. Until now.

"I'm going to call him right after I call Aunt Jo and make sure this is a good day to visit her."

Lil snorted and carried the last of the coasters to the table. "More like you were going to call him after you passed through Warner so he couldn't stop you."

Shandra shoved her hands on her hips. "Why would it matter whether or not Ryan cared if I went to the reservation? He isn't my keeper." That was why she'd kept their relationship at arm's length. She'd had several men over the years who had dictated her life. She wouldn't do that again. She was older and wiser than when she'd lived at home and been a college student.

"I seen the way you've had your nose in your computer. There's something you're digging up. From where I'm at, I see trouble." Lil picked up Lewis. "I'm going to feed the horses."

Chapter Two

Shandra held the phone to her ear and smiled. "Yes, Aunt Jo, I can make the trip easily today. Yes, I know there is a snow storm headed to Northern Idaho, but I'll be headed to Northeast Washington."

"I'll be working at the Community Center until three. You can stop at the center if you get here before that. Otherwise, I'll be home," Josephine Elwood, her father's sister, said.

"I should be at Nespelem before three, it's only a three-hour drive in good weather. I'm figuring four hours today." Shandra didn't worry about weather in her Jeep.

"We'll be looking forward to your visit. I have to go or I'll be late for work."

"Have a good day," Shandra said and hung up. The next call wouldn't be as easy. Ryan knew why she wanted to visit her family.

To stall, she walked into the kitchen and added more tea to her cup then sat down at the counter. She turned the phone on and found Ryan's number. A deep breath fortified her and she tapped his name.

The phone rang several times and went to voice-mail.

He must be working.

The phone beeped.

"Ryan, this is Shandra. I'm headed to Nespelem for a couple of days. I'll text you when I arrive so you don't worry." She tapped the phone and let the air out of her lungs. That was one bullet she'd dodged.

She cleaned up the kitchen and went into the bedroom to dress and pack clothes for a couple of days. The suitcase was packed and she was dressed when a jazz tune filtered into the bedroom.

Shandra ran into the kitchen, then hesitated to pick the phone up when she saw the caller. Sliding her finger across the screen, she took a deep breath and answered.

"Hello, Ryan."

"What is this about going to Nespelem today? If you wait until the weekend I can take you." His deep voice always soothed her. But his words riled.

"I don't need you to take me to Nespelem. I've made the drive a couple times by myself."

"Not during the type of weather we're having now. There's another storm coming through tomorrow."

"I'll be at Aunt Jo's tomorrow. I won't come home until the storm has passed." Shandra had managed just fine the past seven years without anyone telling her what to do or when to do it.

"Why do you have to go today?" Ryan questioned.

"I had a dream. I have to ask my aunt some questions." She inhaled and slowly let the air out. "Ryan, I can't go on without answers."

"I know. Everyone wants closure, but you can't take the word of an old man who was drinking heavily at the time of your father's death." He blew out a long breath. "Shandra, I looked into the records, what little there were, and no one suspected foul play. It was an accident."

Tears burned behind her eyes. She'd expected Ryan to do his own digging, especially, when he'd suggested she not stir up the past. Her last dream remained vivid in her mind. She couldn't ignore the fact, it meant something.

"The authorities wouldn't have looked for anything other than an accident the way it happened. Ella was in my dream last night. I can't explain it, but I know he was murdered. I just have to piece it all together." Shandra brushed the tear sliding down her cheek away. "I'll let you know when I get to the reservation." She touched the off button and stood in the kitchen watching snowflakes float by the window.

I have to know the truth. She shoved her phone in her purse and returned to the bedroom to get her suitcase.

Once everything was stowed in the Jeep, she turned to Lil who stood ten feet from the vehicle, one hand on Sheba's scruff.

Shandra knelt in front of Sheba. "Be good. I'll be back in a few days. You'll have so much fun playing in the snow you won't even know I'm gone."

Sheba stared at her with sad puppy-dog eyes and licked her cheek.

"Don't make me feel bad. This is something I need to do." Shandra stood, wiped the slobber from her cheek, and peered into Lil's eyes. "I'll keep in touch, but I should be back in three days. When the kiln shuts off just leave the vase in it. We are ahead on the coasters, but the lodge sent an order for one hundred. They want to be prepared for the Christmas shoppers. If you could box them up and deliver the order today or tomorrow that would be a big help."

Lil nodded. "I'll deliver them this afternoon."

"Thanks. See you on Thursday." Shandra climbed into her Jeep, waved at Lil with Lewis slung around her neck and Sheba sitting beside her, and put the vehicle in gear.

Chapter Three

Three and a half hours later, Shandra drove through Grand Coulee, over the bridge, and onto the Colville Reservation. This was only the third time in her life she'd visited here even though half of her heritage called this area home since 1885.

Nearing the agency, she glanced to her left and bobbed her head to the six metal root diggers, images of women digging roots as in days past, and continued on toward the Colville Agency. The snow had disappeared an hour earlier. The wind blew but the roads were clear and the traveling easy.

The agency had buildings scattered on both sides of the highway. To the right stood the tribal gas station and trading post. Behind it other new and old buildings that dealt with the needs of the people on the reservation scattered along narrow asphalt and dirt roads. To the left of the highway the community center sat looking inviting. Aunt Jo worked in the cheerful building as the community center coordinator.

Shandra turned left and parked in the small gravel parking lot in front of the center. She'd never set foot in the community center. Eighteen years earlier when she'd stayed with Ella, the old woman had kept her on the family horse ranch up the Nespelem River.

A half a dozen teenagers burst through the double doors, bounded down the stairs, and piled into a small car newer than her Jeep. She watched the back end of the vehicle fishtail as the driver gunned the car pulling out of the gravel parking lot. Shaking her head at their disregard for safety, she walked up the steps and entered the building.

The entry was well lit from the large windows in the front of the building. Posters and Native American Art hung on the walls. An easel had a listing of activities for the month. An elder sat on the couch to her left. He nodded but didn't smile. Straight ahead was a long, sloped walkway. She contemplated whether to walk down when a group of men in their twenties, joking and jostling one another, appeared from the depths of the corridor.

"Excuse me?" she asked.

The joking stopped. All dropped their gaze to their feet, except for the tallest of the group.

"Yeah?" he asked.

"I'm looking for my aunt. Josephine Elwood."

The young man's cheeks reddened and his gaze lit everywhere but her face. "She's down the hall over there. Fourth door."

Shandra wondered about the way they all shifted their feet and hurried on by her. She shrugged and followed the young man's directions. She didn't remember Aunt Jo as being a hard nose, but from the way the young men acted it made her wonder.

The fourth door on the left stood ajar. Shandra knocked and walked in. Aunt Jo looked up from her seat behind a computer monitor.

"Shandra. You made good time." Aunt Jo waved her hand at the computer. "I have to finish filling out next month's schedule. Take a seat or wander through that door and grab a drink out of the little fridge."

Shandra dropped her purse in a chair and wandered into the next room. From the stacked folders, boxes of decorations, scrap paper, stickers, and glue sticks it was a store room of sorts. She found the small fridge and grabbed a bottle of water. Returning to the other room, she found Aunt Jo frowning at the monitor screen.

"Anything I can help you with?" Shandra asked.

"No. This is an old system and things don't always save as they should." She glanced up and smiled. "I called several cousins. We're all meeting at Velma's house for dinner tonight. I thought it was time you really met your family."

Shandra sat down and took a sip of her water before answering. She hadn't planned on a family reunion. "That's nice. I didn't come here to get reacquainted with family. I came to learn more about my father."

Jo glanced up from the monitor. "This is the best way. Edward's family will all be there and you can ask them anything, but be prepared. You've stayed away for many years and there will be those who don't trust you. You've lived as a White man. The only time you showed interest in your heritage was at my mother's funeral. The elders will question your motives for asking questions of the dead, now, so many years later."

Shandra had expected there would be members of the family who would take their time determining if she should receive answers to her questions.

"I know I've not been a good member of this family. At first it wasn't by my choice, then later, I wasn't sure how you would all accept me." Shandra opened her water and took a swallow.

Aunt Jo smiled. "Once they see you want to be part of the family, I'm sure they will come around." She clicked a few more buttons on the keyboard and stood. "There. I'm done for the day."

Shandra stood, slipping her purse over her shoulder. "What all do you do here?"

Aunt Jo waved a hand. "I set up all the events, coordinate the use of the facilities, and make sure there are people in charge of opening and closing the facilities."

"That's a lot of juggling I bet," Shandra waited for Jo to put on her coat and grab her purse from the back room.

"It is. But if there is no one to set up events and make the kids feel at home here, they will go out and drink and do drugs. I try to have events that will appeal to all ages, and hopefully, keep them informed on how to live a clean life." Aunt Jo closed the door and locked it. She slipped the key into her purse and headed to the front door. Instead of walking to the door, she turned down the hallway on the opposite side of the sloping corridor.

"Down there," she pointed to the tunnel the young men had walked up, "is the gym. It is always busy whether it's a basketball practice, game, tournament, or a speaker or other event." She continued down the short hallway.

Large windows looked down into the gym. There were more men, the age of the ones she'd encountered, playing basketball.

"Basketball is the main entertainment around here. Families play families and there is much rivalry." Aunt Jo shook her head. "It's not good to have such feelings for other families." She shrugged. "That's what happens when so many different tribes are living in one place."

"How many different tribes are there?" Shandra asked. She'd looked them up on the computer and hadn't given much thought to whether or not they would get along.

"Twelve tribes live on this reservation. They get along for the most part, but there is always bad feelings, jealousy, when a person or family of one tribe has good fortune. Those that only see bad try to bring down the ones who see promise."

"That sounds like outside the reservation. There are some who don't strive to do better, yet they talk poorly of those that do," Shandra said.

Aunt Jo nodded. "The people and tribes of the reservation are like anywhere. You have those that work hard, get a good education, and come back to try and help. Then you have the ones that feel they have been wronged and instead of trying to change things, they drink or do drugs, don't finish school, and continue to complain. They try to forget their hardships by using drugs or drinking themselves into a stupor, or committing suicide. We have a high rate of suicides, mostly in our youth."

Shandra had heard stories about drugs and alcohol on reservations but had thought people were stereotyping and just wanted to slur the Native Americans. "Isn't it against the culture to take one's own life?"

Aunt Jo nodded. "But when they are high, they forget about traditions and honor. They only want out of the depressing life they see in front of them."

Shandra followed her aunt out into the parking lot. The sun was already drifting to the horizon.

"Follow me. I'll take you to Velma's. She'll be glad to see you." Aunt Jo unlocked the door of a newer pickup, grasped the hand hold, and pulled herself in.

Shandra unlocked her Jeep and followed Aunt Jo out of the parking lot, back to the highway, and left to Nespelem.

The streets were narrow but mostly paved. Some houses and yards were neat and tidy while others could use a coat of paint and repairs and had several old and new vehicles cluttering the yards.

Shandra tried to remember Velma as they wound through the streets. What she remembered of the woman came from their meeting at Ella's funeral. Velma was her father's cousin. She was a bit older than Shandra's father, tall, wide shoulders, and big hands. She was also at the seven drums ceremony. Shandra scanned her memory. Yes, Velma, one of her daughters, and Shandra were the only Higheagles at the ceremony.

Did that mean Velma would understand Ella

coming to her in dreams?

Aunt Jo turned into a short drive that led to a large, tidy house. A small barn with three horses in the corral stood to the side of the house. There were already half a dozen cars parked in front of the lawn and house.

Shandra parked next to Jo. Her aunt smiled and waved her to follow.

Shandra stepped out of the Jeep and raised her phone. "Just a minute. I need to let my friend know I made the trip fine." She texted Ryan she was at the reservation and then called Lil. Lil didn't answer. Shandra left a brief message telling her she was with her aunt.

Jo stood on the porch waiting for Shandra to join her.

Hurrying up the walkway, Shandra shoved the phone in the pocket on the side of her purse.

"Don't be nervous. Velma has been anxious to visit with you ever since mother's ceremony." Aunt Jo put an arm around Shandra's shoulders and knocked on the door.

Shandra's heart raced. She needed answers but had a feeling she would be as novel to her relatives as they were to her.

Chapter Four

The large woman Shandra remembered as Velma answered the door. Her black hair, streaked with gray, hung loose around her shoulders. She stood a good head taller than Shandra and her shoulders filled the door opening.

"Come in! The weather is getting colder." Velma ushered them into a brightly lit living room. Several women Shandra's age and older sat on the couch and a chair. Two young men leaned against a doorway.

Shandra stopped scanning the room. The taller of the two had been the one from the community center who'd answered her question. The minute he realized she'd recognized him, his cheeks darkened.

That was why he'd hurried out of the center. He'd realized she was family.

Velma took their coats and started the

introductions.

"This is my daughter, Wendy, you should remember her from Aunt Minnie's ceremony." Velma placed a hand on the woman sitting in the chair by herself.

Shandra nodded and smiled at her cousin.

"This is my sister, Clarice, and her daughter, Sky." Velma motioned to the two larger women on one end of the couch.

Shandra nodded, smiled, and said, "It's nice to meet you."

"And these two are," Velma waved her hand at the other two younger, smaller women on the couch, "your cousins, Jackie and Sylvia."

Shandra nodded, smiled, and said, "I'm pleased to finally meet my cousins when there is time to visit."

Velma moved to the young men standing in the doorway. "These are Jo's boys. Coop and Andy."

"We've already met," Shandra said, smiling.

The two eyed her suspiciously, then smiled.

"You have? When?" Velma asked.

"At the center," Coop, the tallest said.

"Yeah, we were leaving when she arrived," added Andy. He was a head shorter and stouter than his tall, thin brother.

"I hope you behaved yourselves," Jo said, narrowing her eyes at her sons.

"They did," Shandra said and received wide grins from the two.

Aunt Jo took hold of Shandra's arm. "Come in and sit," she said, pulling Shandra to the last stuffed chair. Jo sat in the folding chair next to Shandra.

All eyes were on her. Shandra smiled even though her first instinct was to flee. The churning in her stomach resembled her first day of grade school, before her mother started using Adam, her stepfather's, last name when she registered Shandra for school.

Velma arrived with a cup of steaming hot coffee. "Nothing like a cup of coffee on a cold day like this," she said, pulling up another folding chair on Shandra's left.

"Thank you," Shandra muttered before taking a sip. She wasn't a coffee drinker but she wasn't going to refuse something warm to hold in her hands.

"Josephine said you had some questions for us about Edward," Velma said, leaning toward Shandra.

Velma didn't move into conversations as slowly as Shandra remembered Ella and her friends had when Shandra had visited the summer she was thirteen.

"Y-yes." Shandra scanned the eager faces. She directed her attention to the older women. The ones who were alive when her father followed the rodeos, became married, and died. "I ran into an old cowboy who rode the circuit with father. Since I don't remember much about my father, I asked the cowboy questions." She smiled. "This cowboy, Phil Seeton, had only good things to say about father." Her heart filled with the memories of Daddy. His kindness. "How father always treated others with respect." She frowned. "Even the ones who weren't nice to him." Phil had told her stories of how some of the Caucasian cowboys had harassed the Indians on the circuit.

"Your father was a good man. A good Nez Perce," Velma said, nodding her head.

Clarice and Jo also nodded their heads.

"Is that why you're here? To find your roots by starting with your father?" Velma asked.

"Yes, and no." Shandra took a sip of coffee to stall for time to find the right words.

Everyone watched her. She didn't want to tell everyone about her dreams and Ella coming to her in them. Velma and Wendy would understand the significance, but Jo had told her Clarice didn't care for her sister's belief in the seven drum religion.

"I am interested in my roots. But I'm more interested in justice." She peered into Velma's eyes. *She knew!* Shandra stared into the depths of the woman's eyes and saw the same thing she witnessed in her dreams. The horses in a circle staring down at her father.

Velma nodded and took her hand. "I've been waiting for you to seek the truth."

"What are you two talking about?" Aunt Jo asked, breaking the connection Shandra felt with Velma.

"Your brother didn't die from an accident," Velma stated, releasing Shandra's hand and peering at Aunt Jo.

"What? No. It was ruled an accident." Jo shook her head as if her head thought one thing and her heart another.

Clarice stood. "Did you bring this poor girl here to trample on her heart to prove your visions?"

"Velma didn't bring me here. Talking to Mr. Seeton brought me here and has had me digging into the past trying to find the truth." Shandra motioned with her hands for Clarice to sit. "Mr. Seeton believes my father didn't have an accident. He said the horse father drew that day was an easy ride for him, that he shouldn't have fallen off. And it was well known that same horse would stomp a man if he landed on the ground."

Shandra faced her aunt. "Were you at the rodeo that day? Did you see it? Or do you know of someone that was there that I could talk to?" Now that her intentions were out in the open, she wasn't leaving here until she'd talked with anyone who might know something.

Aunt Jo shook her head. "I wasn't there. Your mother had asked me to watch you for the weekend." She patted Shandra's head. "We so rarely saw you even before your father's death, I didn't say no."

Guilt gnawed at Shandra. The years since graduating high school, when she was legally free to do whatever she'd wanted, she'd stayed away from the side of her family who wanted her.

But she latched onto the conversation. "How often had mother left me with you during rodeos?"

"That was the first, and last, time." Jo's eyes held sadness. "We didn't see you again until that summer you showed up without warning." She smiled. "Your ella, was so happy you came. She talked about your visit for years afterward and wondered when you'd come back."

The guilt slapped Shandra again. She took Jo's hands. "I'm sorry I didn't find my way sooner. I would have enjoyed learning more about my past from Ella." She glanced at Velma. "And other family members."

"You're here now, that's what counts," Velma said. She waved her hand at Coop. "Bring me that pad and pen sitting on the kitchen counter."

Coop disappeared then returned. In three steps, he

stood beside Velma. "This one? Looks like you lost to Clarice again. Ays," he said and received a swat from Velma.

"She cheats." Velma glared at her sister.

"How can I cheat playing dominoes?" Clarice asked.

Velma humphed and took the pad and pen. "I'll make a list of names of people who you should talk to." She scribbled a few names, then stared at Jo. "Do you think she should talk with Charlie Frank?"

"Who is he?" Shandra asked. The name sounded a bit familiar, but she wasn't sure why.

Aunt Jo scrunched her face. "He was a Colville who also did rodeo and always tried to make Edward look bad."

"He once—" Velma said.

"Charlie hated—" Clarice said at the same time as Velma.

Shandra held up her hand. "One at a time, please."

Velma nodded to her sister.

"Charlie hated Edward since first or second grade," Clarice said. "Those two had a competition over everything they did. Whether it was first to sharpen a pencil or the fastest in a foot race."

"Why did Charlie hate my father?" Shandra asked.

"Jealousy," said Clarice.

Aunt Jo nodded. "Your father had the gift of talking to the horse. Understanding them. He trained his first horse when he was ten. Charlie wanted to train horses to run races. But he didn't have the touch. Or the patience. Edward caught Charlie forcing a horse to do something it wasn't ready for. He stopped Charlie and

30

told Charlie's uncle, who owned the horse, and Charlie wasn't allowed to touch his uncle's racing stock again."

"If Charlie wanted to train race horses why was he on the rodeo circuit?" Shandra was filing all the information away for later. She'd type it all up on her tablet when she retired for the night.

"He saw the rodeo circuit as a way to make money to buy his own racing stock," Velma said.

"Was he that good?" Shandra hadn't seen his name mentioned in any of the newspapers she'd read while following the story about her father's death.

"No. He didn't make money from the rodeos. Another thing that made him angry with your father. Edward placed high enough in rankings to pick up a check at every rodeo."

The pride in Aunt Jo's voice tugged at Shandra. Jo had loved her brother and was proud of him.

"Then how did he buy that ranch and all those race horses?" Coop asked, the first of the younger generation to join in the conversation.

"What ranch? Does he live on the reservation?" Shandra wanted to meet this man who disliked her father.

"He has a ranch up out of Omak," Velma said. Her brows scrunched together. "It was about a month after Edward's death that Charlie bought that land up there."

"How did he get the money?" Shandra asked, her mind already clicking through the government agencies she would need to access to find out more about his ranch.

"You could see if my Bud knows," Clarice said.

"Bud's her husband. He'll be here in an hour for

dinner." Velma stood. "I have some things to take care of before we can eat. Wendy would you keep Shandra company while Clarice, Jo, and I get the food ready?"

Velma didn't wait for her daughter's reply before heading out of the room with the two older women in her wake.

Chapter Five

Shandra spent the next hour trying to keep up a conversation with Wendy and the other young women while her mind was categorizing the things she needed to do next in her investigation.

During that time, old and young men and women, and all ages of children, started shuffling through the front door. Before long the living room was full of people standing and sitting. The noise level made it hard to talk to anyone. Shandra stood and headed to the door into the kitchen. Wendy had introduced her to each person who arrived, but her mind was spinning with names and how they were related. The older men were the ones she wanted to talk with. They, however, kept their distance, sending furtive glances her way until she'd make eye contact. Then they'd become engrossed in visiting with one another.

In the kitchen Jo, Velma, and Clarice were lining pots, pans, and casserole dishes up on the counter with a pile of paper plates and plastic utensils on the counter at the end near the kitchen entrance.

"You didn't have to go to all this trouble because I'm visiting," Shandra said.

All three women turned and stared at her.

"You buzzed in and out so fast after Mother's funeral we didn't have a chance to bring everyone together to meet you," Aunt Jo said, waving a large serving spoon.

The guilt twisted Shandra's insides. "I hope all of you can forgive my staying away. I'd spent so many years without extended family that I didn't see a need to perhaps stir up trouble."

"Trouble? What kind of trouble?" Velma asked, ramming a potato masher up and down in a large pot.

Shandra wasn't sure how to say it. "Not being brought up as the rest of you were, I didn't want to be stereotyped."

Clarice stared at her. "Just because you were raised by that snooty mother of yours who looked at all of us like we were going to scalp her, doesn't mean we believed you'd turn your back on your heritage."

"That step you made when you were thirteen showed us you'd be back. You'd want to know more." Jo spread out her arms. "And here you are."

"Yes, here I am." Shandra motioned to a salad that looked like it needed tossed. "Would you like me to stir that up?"

Aunt Jo smiled. "That would be nice."

They finished up the last of the meal preparations and Clarice headed into the other room to let people know the food was ready.

Shandra took this time to sidle up to Velma. Keeping her voice low, so Aunt Jo couldn't hear, she asked, "I would like to talk with you privately tomorrow."

Velma nodded. "Come by any time. I'm home all day."

Nodding, Shandra moved to the plates and picked one up. After filling her plate with salad, a noodle casserole, and meatballs, she glanced at the long line of people starting along the counter adding food to their plates.

Aunt Jo touched her arm. Her plate was full as well. "Come on. There's tables set up in the barn."

They didn't put their coats on, but after the heat of the kitchen, the crisp evening air was welcome. Shandra followed her aunt into the barn. There were sheets of wood on wooden saw horses and bales of hay along the make-shift tables like benches.

"The boys set this up this afternoon," Aunt Jo said, sliding onto a bale.

Shandra sat on the other end of the bale. When the first person entered the barn she realized Jo had seated them to not miss a single person entering.

Jo started telling her names, how they were related, and what they did. "That's Bud," she said when Clarice's husband stepped through the door. "Bud! Bud, over here!" her aunt called out.

The man was in his early sixties. His long, graying hair hung in two braids down his chest. He was average height, stocky, with a long, wide nose, and dark eyes. Bud nodded to Shandra and sat at the table across from Jo.

"Bud, this is my niece, Shandra Higheagle." Jo nodded to Shandra.

"I'm pleased to meet you," Shandra said, holding out her hand to shake.

He grasped her hand and shook once. "You're Edward's daughter. The potter."

Shandra nodded and smiled. "Yes. I didn't realize you knew that much about me."

Bud picked up his fork and chewed on some lettuce. He set the fork down and nodded. "We like to keep tabs on those outside the reservation who promote the old ways."

Shaking her head, Shandra peered into the man's eyes. "I don't promote the old ways. In fact, probably far from it."

"You form the earth into useable and artistic pots. Pottery is something our forefathers did to help with their survival." Bud nodded and chewed on another bite. He swallowed. "You did not forget your roots, even when your mother tried to wring them from you."

Shandra smiled. Her mother would cringe if she knew Shandra's passion of making vases from clay was a part of her heritage calling to her. Which brought up another question.

"Mother has always been anti-Indian and you have all made comments that make me wonder why she married my father." She studied Aunt Jo and Bud's faces.

The two made eye contact. Aunt Jo sighed, making

her chest expand and then deflate. "We never wanted to have the truth told to you, but you're old enough to know." Jo put down her plastic fork and took Shandra's hand. "Edward, your father, told me that he was pretty sure your mother only flirted and slept with him to get back at your stepfather."

"Adam? He was mother's boyfriend before my father?" Shandra's brain started flashbacks. That was why her mother and Adam had never talked about knowing one another before her father's death. They didn't want her to know…What?

"Then why did mother marry father? She could have given me up and married Adam."

"Your father told her you would not be put up for adoption or taken from her body." Jo closed her eyes briefly.

Shandra understood what she meant. "Was my mother prepared to have an abortion?"

"She had threatened Edward with that if he didn't keep quiet about the pregnancy. She knew she couldn't pass you off as Adam's if you came out with Indian characteristics." Aunt Jo smiled. "And you did. You were the prettiest Indian baby."

"That still doesn't explain the marriage." Shandra turned her attention to Bud. He was fiddling with the food on his plate.

"Your grandmother told your mother if she didn't marry Edward, your grandmother would ruin it for Celeste to ever marry another. That they could try marriage and if it didn't work, she could walk away. But you were to remain with your father." Aunt Jo shook her head. "Mother should not have forced the two together. I don't know if she saw something and thought they could make it or she hoped your mother would learn to love our ways and your father."

Shandra shoved her plate to the center of the table. The din of many voices, children laughing and crying rose up to roar in her ears. Could Ella's forcing her parents together have caused her father's death?

Chapter Six

Shandra followed the red taillights of Aunt Jo's pickup out the dirt road up the Nespelem River to the Higheagle horse ranch. Her great-great-grandfather had received federal trust acres and the family had since added non-trust acres making the Higheagle ranch near a thousand acres. On her visit when she was thirteen, she'd enjoyed learning how to listen to the horses when working with and riding them. On her stepfather's ranch in Montana, the horses were treated as a machine. A means to get the cattle rounded up out of the mountains or to use at branding. While at the Higheagle ranch, Shandra learned horses were creatures who deserved respect and admiration. The animal had taken care of the Nez Perce for centuries.

Aunt Jo's truck drove through the open gate to the house and barnyard.

She noticed Coop's fancy truck parked to the side
of the lean-to Aunt Jo drove her pickup under. Shandra
parked on the far side of Coop's truck. She didn't know
if she'd be leaving in the morning before either of them
but didn't want to block their way.

Shandra stepped out of her Jeep, opened the back
door, and grabbed her overnight bag.

"You travel light," Aunt Jo said. "Or you were only
planning a short trip."

"I travel light. There are enough clothes for three
days. I figured that was all I'd need to gather enough
information to continue my search back at my ranch."
Shandra pulled the overnight bag out of the car and shut
the door.

She fell in step beside her aunt. They walked into
the door off the carport.

Uncle Martin, Jo's husband, stood with his back to
them looking into the refrigerator. "Did you bring me
anything, Josie?" he asked without turning around.

Jo patted her husband on the back. "Sorry. There
wasn't a crumb left when everyone filled their plates."

Martin grunted. "Coop and Andy thought there
might have been some of your aunt Dottie's casserole
left." He faced his wife and closed the fridge door.

She laughed. "You hate that."

"But I'm hungry enough I could eat it now." He
winked at Shandra.

Uncle Martin and Aunt Jo had lived at the ranch
with Ella. At thirteen she hadn't found the way they
joked with one another and the children as endearing as
she did as an adult.

"I see the guest of honor is here." He stepped

forward, pulling Shandra into a bear hug.

"It's good to see you again, Uncle Martin." Shandra couldn't hug him back because she had her overnight bag in one hand and her purse in the other. She stepped out of his embrace. "It's been a long day."

"Coop? Coop!" Aunt Jo called into the other room.

Pounding steps on the stairs, brought Coop ducking into the kitchen. "Yeah?"

"Show Shandra to your room," Aunt Jo said.

"I don't need to put anyone out of their bed," Shandra protested.

"It's okay. Andy has bunks in his room. I'll just hang my feet over the end and make him smell them all night. Ays." Coop winked and looked a lot like his father, before he spun to the door and waved for her to follow.

"Good night," Shandra said, following her cousin out of the kitchen, through the large living room, which looked much as she remembered it, and up the stairs. To her surprise and pleasure, Coop's room was the guest room she'd slept in that summer she'd ran away to her heritage.

"Thank you. I am sorry to put you out of your room," she said, stepping through the threshold and finding the room neat and tidy. A double bed took up the length of the far wall that had a window. The wall to her right held a desk with one of the newest computers on the market.

"You can hop on the internet if you want," Coop said, obviously reading her interest in his computer as her wanting to get online.

"If I can't get a good signal with my tablet, I will

borrow it if you don't mind." She set her bag on the floor next to the bed.

"Andy has one in his room I can use if I need to check something out." Coop headed to the door. He stopped and faced the room. "Mom is real excited about your visit." His gaze dropped to the floor. "If this is a one-time thing, don't stay too long." He stepped backward, ducked into the hall, and closed the door.

Shandra stared at the door. He was worried his mother would be hurt. His concern endeared him to Shandra. *I don't have plans to hurt anyone. I just need the truth.*

Jazz tunes tinkled from her phone. Pulling it out of her side pocket, she noticed she'd missed one call from Lil and two from Ryan.

The screen showed Ryan's name. She slid her finger across the screen.

"Hello."

"I got your text, but wanted to hear how your visit is going," Ryan said.

She smiled. He was concerned about her being accepted. She'd told him about the separation from her father's side of the family.

"Aunt Jo and Uncle Martin have always been good to me. Jo and my cousin Velma had a dinner in my honor tonight. There were so many relatives, I'll never be able to remember their names."

Ryan smiled at the phone. He'd been afraid she'd run into resistance at the reservation and come back frustrated. Even though he'd told her many times her father's death was decades old and would be hard to find information about.

"You visit a time or two and you'll keep them straight." He had been against her trip to the reservation only because she would dredge up the past and if a murder had been committed, could become a target.

"I'm not as confident as you." She paused. "I discovered there was another Indian who was rodeoing the same time as father and the two didn't get along."

"Shandra, you know whatever you find out, I can't do a thing about until there is solid proof." This was the frustrating part. Hearing all the information she dug up and worrying about her safety.

"I know. I was hoping you could do a little checking on him?"

He heard what sounded like bed springs squeak. Shandra must have sat on a bed. "You have to be tired from the trip and meeting all those people. How about I call you back tomorrow?"

"That's fine. Then you can tell me what you find out about Charlie Frank. He is Colville, rodeoed, and has a ranch up by Omak."

His instincts kicked in. "You aren't heading to Omak by yourself."

"I can't ask anyone to go with me. They have their own lives to lead."

Ryan wouldn't let this slide. "If you decide to go to Omak, take someone with you. There has to be a cousin or someone who would like to get to know you better or need a ride that direction."

"I can't impose on—"

"It's not imposing. It's for your own safety." Ryan wasn't going to hang up until she agreed to take someone with her. He wasn't convinced her father was murdered, but he'd learned to trust her dreams. If this Frank person did kill her father, she'd be walking into trouble.

"I'm just going to ask questions about my father, you know 'a wanting to learn more about him' stage of my life. I won't bring up I don't think it was an accident." Shandra sighed. "I'm tired. I'll call you tomorrow."

The phone went silent. Ryan pulled out the notepad he kept in his shirt pocket and flipped through the pages to Josephine Elwood's phone number. Shandra may not think she needed company but he would make sure she wasn't alone.

Chapter Seven

Shandra rose early the next day. She felt refreshed and was happy to have a full night of sleep without Ella visiting her dreams. Sitting on the bed, she dialed Lil's phone.

Three rings and Lil answered. "Mornin'."

"Good morning. How is Sheba this morning?" Shandra asked, starting off with the most important thing on her mind.

"She likes when you're gone and she can sleep in here with us," Lil said.

Shandra could hear Sheba panting in the background and the purr of Lewis who was most likely draped over Lil's shoulders.

"Good. I'm glad she likes having sleepovers. The horses all well?"

"Yes, ma'am. We had about four more inches

dumped on us yesterday, but I got them coasters to the resort and back in time to put them in stalls."

"I don't know what I'd do without you," Shandra said, and meant every word of it. The woman was the perfect fit for what she needed in the way of help.

"Remember that come Christmas," Lil joked.

"I will," Shandra laughed. "Did the kiln turn off last night?" She knew Lil always followed her orders when it came to the pottery, but this was something new. Something she hoped to wow the judges with at the next show. To win a prize at the New Mexico show was a real coup for a potter.

"I checked it at ten and it was still going, but when I tottered out there about midnight it had just turned off."

"That sounds like the right amount of time. Just leave it set in the kiln," she instructed.

"I won't touch it. You coming back today?"

"No. I'm headed up to Omak to talk to someone. My plan is to be back tomorrow." Ryan's conversation had been running around in her head as she fell asleep last night. She woke with the gnawing feeling she should probably heed his warning.

"Okay, we'll be here. I'll take the tractor and plow out tomorrow morning and clear the road of snow."

"That's a good idea. See you tomorrow." Shandra hit the off button, tucked the phone in her purse, slung the purse over her shoulder, and headed downstairs.

The kitchen was full of activity. Jo stood at the stove, flipping pancakes. Martin was washing his hands at the sink. Coop and Andy sat at the table arguing about basketball. This was the type of family Shandra had dreamed of having while growing up an only child in a house that had a housekeeper. Her breakfasts had been eaten in the kitchen while the housekeeper cleaned up the dishes from Adam's morning meal. Her mother never ate more than toast and coffee for breakfast. And that was usually after Shandra headed to school.

"You're up! I was just getting ready to send someone up to see if you were sleeping in," Aunt Jo said, smiling and placing a large plate of pancakes on the table.

"I was on the phone with Lil, my help, checking on my dog and horses." Shandra hung her purse on a vacant chair and sat.

"What are your plans today?" Martin asked.

"I want to visit with Velma before I head to Omak and talk to Charlie Frank." Shandra shook her head when Jo placed a cup of coffee in front of her plate. "I'm not a fan of coffee."

"I need to go to Omak. Can I bum a ride? It will save me gas." Coop peered at her with dark brown eyes.

"What do you need to do there?" She found it too much of a coincidence he needed to go to Omak when Ryan had been insistent someone go with her.

"They have a sports store there. I need a new pair of basketball shoes." He held up a foot that had to be close to a size thirteen.

"I guess it's hard to find your size around here." The thought of getting to know him better overrode the feeling she had been manipulated by Ryan.

Aunt Jo placed a cup of tea in front of Shandra. "Thank you. I didn't have the heart yesterday to tell Velma I didn't like coffee."

Jo smiled. "She makes a strong cup of coffee anyway. I'm surprised you didn't make a face when you sipped her brew."

"The smell told me it was strong so I barely took a sip. I mainly held it for the warmth." Shandra looked down at the plate piled high with pancakes, bacon, and scrambled eggs that Aunt Jo placed in front of her. "I can't eat this much," she said.

Martin sat down opposite her. He tipped his head toward Andy. "What you don't eat, he'll clean up."

Andy nodded as he scooped a forkful of pancake into his mouth.

Shandra laughed and dug into her breakfast. This was what had been missing in her childhood. A pang of grief clenched her chest. She could have had this fifteen years ago if she'd sought her family when she'd left home at eighteen.

"What's wrong?" Jo asked, sitting next to Shandra, placing a hand on her arm.

"Nothing. Just wishing I hadn't stayed away from all of you so long." Tears burned behind her eyes. She'd missed out on learning things from Ella and getting to know the side of her family she most connected with.

"Well, you're here now." Jo hugged her and Martin nodded his head. She glanced at the boys. They were grinning and nodding. For the first time in a very long time, she felt as if she were home.

"Thank you. Next time I come, I'll bring my friend, Ryan. He's been pestering me about learning more about my heritage." Shandra picked up her tea. She noticed a look that went between Jo and Martin.

"What was that?" she asked.

"What?" Jo asked, rising from her chair and moving to the sink.

Shandra peered into Martin's eyes. "Did Ryan contact you?"

"Me?" Martin's eyes widened. He shook his head. "I haven't talked to anyone but those of this household."

Shandra had a feeling Ryan had called here after talking to her. But she wasn't going to find out from Martin or Jo. She smiled at Coop. She'd get it out of him on the way to Omak. She stood.

"Thank you for breakfast. Coop, get your things if you're going with me. You can find something to do while I visit with Velma." Shandra faced her aunt. "We'll be back for dinner. Depending on what I learn in Omak, I'll either stay another day or leave tomorrow." She hugged her aunt. "But I'll be back to visit soon."

"You know once you say a thing like that you can't go back on your word," Aunt Jo said, stepping back and peering into Shandra's eyes.

"You have my word." Shandra slid her arms into her coat and picked up her purse.

"You know, you carry many traits of your father." Martin pointed to her leather fringed, messenger bag styled purse with beading. "That is very close to the traditional bags we used to carry things."

Shandra smiled. "I know. That's why I like it."

Coop loped into the room. "Ready."

"Let's go." Shandra exited the house, drew her coat closer, and headed to her Jeep. The gray skies loomed low and oppressive. "Will it snow?"

"No. We rarely get snow. If we do, it melts right

away." Coop climbed into her passenger seat. "Nice!"

"Your pickup is newer than my Jeep," Shandra said, buckling up and backing out to the driveway.

Coop ran his hand over her dash. "Didn't you get this when you turned eighteen?"

Shandra stared at him. "No. I bought this when I made enough from my pottery to afford a new car."

"But you got a new car when you turned eighteen," he said, staring at her wide-eyed.

"No. When I was seventeen, I worked for my stepfather and I worked for a neighbor in the summer to buy a 1977 Ford pickup that would haul the two-horse trailer I'd worked for the summer before." She had worked for everything other than the ranch on Huckleberry Mountain. She'd purchased that with money her grandmother on her mother's side had left her.

"You had to work to get your first car? When you live on the rez, when you turn eighteen and have a diploma, you get what we call 'Eighteen Money'. Most go out and buy a car with it." He made the statement like it was a privilege.

"But I've seen how the young people around here drive, and I've seen new cars sitting in yards that look like they've been wrecked." They were on the outskirts of Nespelem. She pointed to the right. "Like that one. How did it get mangled like that?"

Coop smiled. "That was the pickup Rodney Near rolled one night when a group of us were up at Owhi Lake drinking."

Shandra shook her head. "Was anyone hurt in the accident?"

Coop sobered. "Yeah, Rodney had to have pins put in his leg where the truck rolled over it and Debbie was in a coma for a couple of weeks."

"Your mother mentioned how bad drinking and drugs were on the reservation. Do you drink or do drugs?" She asked, not to get him in trouble but to make him see it wasn't the route to go.

"I drink once in a while, but I'm of age." He scowled at her.

"Do you drink until you're stupid?" she asked, pulling into Velma's driveway. She was pleased to see only one car. She presumed it belonged to Velma.

"I'm going to make something of myself. I won't become like Uncle Clyde and some of my friends." His eyes shone with conviction.

"I hope so. Life is too precious to throw it away. What do you want to do for a living?" She turned off the Jeep and turned to Coop.

His gaze lingered on the dash, and his fingers picked at the denim incasing his thigh. "I'd thought about basketball, but then I read some stories about players who hadn't had an education and when they became injured became like the lost Indians on the rez." He glanced at her as if expecting her to belittle his dream.

"Don't you have to go to college to get into pro basketball?" she asked.

"I'm taking online courses right now to get into Washington State."

"Good! Let me know when you make it. What will your major be?" She was happy to hear he planned to get out in the world and get a degree.

51

"Computer science." He smiled.

"That's an excellent choice. The world will be run by computers someday." She opened her door as Velma stepped out onto her porch. The woman waved, then cast a glance at Coop.

Shandra walked around the front of her Jeep and handed the keys to Coop. "Come back and get me in an hour."

"Really?"

"Yes, Really. But I want my Jeep to look just like it does now." She narrowed her eyes.

"It will. Thanks. I didn't want to sit around Velma's pretending I didn't hear what you talked about." He grinned and hustled around to the driver's side.

Shandra grinned, waved to Coop as he backed out of the drive, and headed up the cracked sidewalk to Velma's porch.

"You sure you want that boy driving your Jeep?" Velma asked.

"He'll be fine. I told him to come back in an hour. He's going to Omak with me." Shandra witnessed Velma's brow rise, but she didn't say anything.

"Come on in. I have a pot of tea ready."

Shandra smiled. Aunt Jo must have called and broken the news to Velma that Shandra wasn't a big coffee drinker.

They settled at the kitchen table.

"Why did you want to visit with me this morning?" Velma asked, lifting a cookie to her mouth.

Shandra fidgeted in her seat. Even though her father's cousin knew why she came here, and belonged to the same religion as Ella, she had a hard time telling her what she found so easy to tell Ryan.

"Has Aunt Minnie visited you?" Velma asked.

Shandra sucked in air so fast she choked. Velma patted her back and shoved Shandra's mug of tea toward her. She raised the glass and drank a long soothing swallow.

"How did you know Ella visited me?" Shandra asked.

"That is why she had you attend the ceremony after her funeral. She wanted to know if she could reach you."

Velma said it all so matter-of-factly, Shandra could only take in the information as real.

"Reach me?" She had a feeling she knew what it meant but wanted to hear it from Velma.

"She planned to visit you in dreams." Velma stared at her. "She has, hasn't she?"

"Yes. The first time was when I was mixed up in a murder. The second time was when my friend Lil was suspected of murder, and the third time was when a man was found dead on my property. But lately, she's been showing me Father, mangled, on the ground, and horses peering down at him." She stared into Velma's eyes. Where she'd witnessed the same scene the day before. Today, they were chocolate brown eyes staring back at her.

"That's what brought you here to find out more about your father's death."

"Yes. I'm headed to Omak to talk with Charlie Frank." Shandra drank her tea.

"You do know looking into your father's death, may reveal truths you don't want to know."

Chapter Eight

Shandra peered into Velma's eyes. After the information she'd learned last night about Adam and her mother, she had a pretty good idea what Velma was referring to.

"I'm aware Mother and Father didn't have a marriage of love."

Velma put her mug down. "When did you discover this?"

"I had a feeling when I talked with Mr. Seeton a couple months ago. Then last night Bud and Jo told me how they thought Mother sleeping with an Indian had been her revenge on Adam. That they'd been seeing one another before my conception and the marriage."

Velma nodded. "I told Aunt Minnie to stay out of it. To let it be. But she feared for you. That was why she forced the two to marry. To keep you alive."

Shandra shook her head. "Mother wouldn't have—" She couldn't bring herself to say the word, only because it would have meant her mother wished to kill her. Celeste wasn't much of a mother, but she couldn't see her cold-blooded enough to kill an innocent baby.

"Minnie had a vision. She saw your mother enter a building that had one of the doctors that back then did that sort of thing. Your ella came to me saying we had to stop Celeste. You were to live." Velma took a drink of her tea. "That was when she threatened your mother. Back then Celeste was naïve to our ways and believed Minnie could put a spell on her, like a witch." Velma laughed. "She was easy to tell stories to."

Shandra saw the humor and also understood her mother's fear. That was why she refused to let Shandra see the Higheagles. She'd believed they would teach her daughter heathen ways.

Velma stopped laughing. "What questions will you ask Charlie Frank?"

Setting her cup down, Shandra told Velma of her plan to talk to Charlie without him becoming suspicious of her reasons.

An hour later, Coop walked through the front door. "Ready to go?" he asked, holding out the keys to Shandra.

"I am." Shandra took the keys, hugged Velma, and donned her coat.

"You should make Omak in time for lunch," Velma said, looking over at the round clock on the wall that had the words 'Indian Time' across the middle and had the numbers in all the wrong places.

"Good. I'm hungry," Coop stated and headed to the

front door.

"You're always hungry," Shandra said, following her cousin out of the house and to her Jeep. She made one pass around the vehicle checking for dings and scratches.

"I thought you trusted my driving," Coop said.

Climbing behind the steering wheel, she glanced over at him. His bottom lip was in a pout and his eyes had taken on a sad countenance. Shandra laughed. "I was just making sure someone else hadn't dinged the Jeep while you were parked."

He snapped out of the pout and smiled. "I parked far from any other cars at the Trading Post."

"Were you there the whole time?" she asked, pulling out of Velma's driveway and heading to the highway.

"Sandy Williams was working today."

She could tell by his tone, he was smitten with the girl. "Really? Tell me about Sandy." The next thirty minutes was spent listening to Coop talk about Sandy and all her accomplishments.

"That's the road Charlie lives on," Coop interrupted his dialogue to point at a road to the left that they'd passed.

"Oh! I thought he lived in Omak." Shandra slowed the Jeep, debating whether to turn around or not.

"No. That's the road. We can go on into Omak, eat lunch, get my shoes, and then stop in on the way back," Coop said.

Shandra's stomach growled. "That sounds like a good plan." She continued on to Omak.

***

Murderous Secrets

Two hours later, their bellies full and a new pair of basketball shoes sitting in her back seat, Shandra turned down the lane to Charlie Frank's ranch. As she drove closer to the buildings and paddocks, she wondered if the man still lived here.

"That barn looks like its leaning, and I don't see any horses," she said to Coop. "Are you sure Charlie still lives here?"

"That's the word. He's here but he's been losing races, bets, and horse owners." Coop stared out the passenger window.

She parked in front of a one-level, ranch-style home. The gray walls had curled flakes of paint clinging to them. Grimy windows gave the building an unfriendly nuance. There were two pickups on blocks between the house and the leaning barn.

"I don't see a running vehicle. Do you think he's even here right now?" Shandra opened the door, hesitant to venture farther without consent of the owner.

"He gets a ride from Tommy Lighthorse when he needs to go to town." Coop closed the Jeep door and strode to the front door.

"How come you know so much about Charlie?" Shandra asked, catching up to Coop's long stride.

"Everyone knows about Charlie. He sees himself as an Indian who made it."

Shandra scanned the porch, missing boards, and the cracked beams holding up the porch roof. "I would say he is an Indian who squandered his good fortune."

Coop shrugged and knocked on the door.

Nothing.

He knocked longer and harder.

57

"Who's there?" called a gravelly, slurred voice.

"Coop Elwood."

Shandra raised an eyebrow at how he'd neglected to say her name.

"He wouldn't come if he knew there was a woman standing out here," Coop said.

She nodded. Why would a woman keep Charlie from coming to the door?

A couple of thuds and shuffling steps on the other side of the door and it opened.

A stooped man with gray braids dangling in the air in front of his body, raised fading brown eyes upward. When he still couldn't seem to see Coop's face, he motioned with his hand. "Lean down, so's I can see you are who you say you are."

Coop grinned and bent at his waist, bringing his face into the man's vision.

Charlie grunted and turned. That's when his gaze landed on Shandra's feet.

"Those are fancy boots." Charlie raised his head as best he could and when he peered into Shandra's face he said something in his language.

Shandra glanced at Coop to see if he knew what the man said. He shook his head.

"Mr. Franks, I'm Shandra Higheagle. I've recently connected with my family and heard you knew my father. Since I was so small when he had his accident, I've been talking to people who knew him to discover what kind of a man he was." She reached down, taking his gnarled fingers in her hand and shaking.

"Higheagle. You mean Edward?" he asked, moving slowly into the house.

"Yes. Edward Higheagle," Shandra said, following the shrunken man into a room piled high with horse magazines of all kinds, empty beer cans, and T.V. dinner containers with half-eaten food in them.

Charlie took the only seat in the place that wasn't covered with anything. Once seated he looked her up and down. He nodded. "You have your father's look."

Coop grabbed the back of what looked to be a dining room chair and dumped the contents on the seat to the floor. Four mice scurried out of the pile.

Shandra squeaked, startled by the creatures and the knowledge the man lived in such deplorable conditions.

Coop placed the chair behind her. She glanced at the wooden seat, hoping there wasn't any mouse leavings. As if reading her mind, Coop picked up a newspaper on the top of a stack of magazines and placed it on the seat.

"Thanks," she said under her breath and sat.

"What can you tell me about Edward?" she asked Charlie.

"He was a member of them snooty Nez Perce in Nespelem." Charlie didn't look at her, he stared at a spot on the floor between his stocking clad feet. The big toe on his left foot stuck out a hole in the sock.

Shandra locked gazes with Coop. Charlie was talking about their family. Coop only shook his head, holding his tongue. Her respect for her cousin had been growing with each hour she spent with him.

"When did you first meet Edward?" she asked, deciding to keep it impersonal and perhaps he'd reveal his true feeling rather than try to keep anything from her.

"In grade school. We fought a lot." Charlie nodded his head.

"What did you fight about?"

Charlie wiggled one of his hands. "Everything."

"Why?"

"Because he thought so high of himself and his family. Others said he had the way with horses. But he didn't. They just said that to make people think he was some kind of horse whisperer when he rode horses that bucked everyone else off, but not him."

"So you think it was just a story he could talk to the horses?" This was interesting considering what she'd learned from Bud and others about her father and this man.

"It had to be. Otherwise, he would have rode Loco that day and not been bucked off." Charlie stared into space now. "He should have talked that horse out of bucking if he was so good."

"You were there that day?" Shandra asked, finally feeling like she had a viable witness.

"Yes. I seen him fall. Landed like a sack of potatoes. Didn't even try to get up or move out of the way of Loco's hooves. We all knew what that horse would do if you landed on the ground. You had to move fast so the hazer could get between you and Loco."

"What do you mean, he didn't even try to get out of the way?" Shandra's chest squeezed with fear. She felt as if she were lying on the ground unable to move out from under the striking hooves.

"They say he hit his head. Knocked him out. That's why he didn't move." Charlie looked up at her. "Wish I hadn't been there."

"Why?"

"Wasn't the way I wanted to see him go down." Charlie picked up the beer can next to his chair and guzzled.

"But you did want him to go down?" Shandra asked.

The old man set the can on the table, wiped his shirt sleeve across his mouth, and nodded. "He thought no one could beat him." Charlie half smiled. "Someone did."

"Someone who?" Her heart pounded in her ears. What did this man know?

"The Creator, the rodeo organizers who were getting tired of hearing from the Whites that an Indian was beating them, the rough stock providers being told their stock wasn't rough enough if an Indian could ride them." He swung an arm. "Take your pick. Edward Higheagle made a lot of people look foolish."

Chapter Nine

Shandra drove back to Nespelem with a thousand questions whirling in her mind. Coop remained quiet. Was he also replaying the conversation or was he thinking about his next basketball game? He'd seemed to hang on every word Charlie said, but then hadn't said a word when they returned to the Jeep.

"You can drop me off at the Center if you want. I can catch a ride home after practice." Coop said as they neared the turnoff to the Higheagle ranch.

"Is your mom working today?" Shandra wasn't sure she was ready to reveal anything she'd learned today to anyone just yet. The people Charlie mentioned as having a problem with her father could be her stepfamily.

"She only worked this afternoon. She could be on her way home by now."

The sun had set just as they pulled into Nespelem. That was the problem with winter, the daylight was too short. It was only 4:30, but darkness was descending.

She pulled into the community center parking lot.

"I don't see mom's pickup. She probably headed home by now," Coop said, reaching into the back seat for his new shoes. "Thanks for giving me a ride to Omak." He held the shoes in his lap. "What are you going to do about what Charlie Frank told us?"

"Make some phone calls. Dig a little more." Shandra didn't see any reason to not tell Coop the truth. He'd heard everything she had and had a right to know where the information might take her.

He nodded. "If you need anything dug up from the rez records let me know. I have access from some of the computer work I'm doing for college and for the tribal council."

Shandra smiled. "That's good to know. Thanks."

"See you at the house." He stepped out and closed the door, waving as he trotted into the center.

Shandra pulled out her phone. The signal was better here than at the ranch.

She dialed Lil.

"Evenin'," Lil answered.

"Good evening. Everything going fine there?" Shandra asked.

"Right as rain. Animals are fed and tucked in for the night. I cleaned the studio and the house today. I'll plow the road in the morning." There was a pause. "Are you coming home tomorrow?"

"At this moment, yes. Unless something comes up. But I doubt it will. My cousin can look into things here on the reservation for me." Shandra didn't think pulling Coop in to find information she wasn't privileged to would harm him.

"Are you leavin' in the morning? I want to make sure the road is clear when you come."

"I'll be home by noon. Does that give you enough time?"

"Yep. I'll be out there as soon as the sun's up."

Shandra's lips tugged into a smile. She had no doubt the woman would be out there at the crack of dawn. "See you tomorrow." Tapping the off button, she then touched her contacts and tapped Ryan's name.

The phone rang twice.

"Good evening, Shandra," he said. The tone told her he was smiling.

"Evening to you, Detective Greer." She was used to the flutter in her belly when he spoke to her that way. It was a sure sign she was getting closer to committing to a relationship with him. But after her last two fiascos she was taking her time with Ryan. She wanted to know him inside and out to make sure he didn't have a hidden side to him like her high school boyfriend and Professor Landers.

"When are you coming home?" Ryan asked.

"Tomorrow."

"Perfect! I have the day off. How about hanging around in Warner with me. I'll buy you lunch and dinner if you want to stay that late."

His enthusiasm was hard to ignore.

"I would love to have lunch and spend some time with you, but I'd like to get home before dark. Can I take a rain check on the dinner?" She would have loved to spend the entire day with him in his environment. They had mostly spent time together in Huckleberry or at her ranch, never where she could meet his friends and learn more about him.

"What time will you be here?"

She laughed. "If I leave at eight I can be there by ten. Is that early enough?"

"No. But it will do. Warner put up the Christmas decorations on the street yesterday."

He sounded excited about Christmas. She usually spent her Christmas going to the local family shelter and handing out small gifts and necessities to the women and children. Helping battered women regain their respect was an important goal of hers.

"I'll get there as close to ten as I can." And I'll wait until then to discuss what I learned.

"I'm on duty. I'll see you tomorrow."

The phone went silent. A day spent with Ryan in an environment where she didn't have to worry about people making assumptions about their relationship. She loved Huckleberry and the residents, but they were too nosy when it came to her and Ryan.

She called Lil back, telling her she'd be hanging out in Warner most of the day but to expect her before dark.

Then she started up her Jeep and headed back to Nespelem and up the Nespelem River. Her thoughts lingered on the conditions Charlie Frank lived in and how he could have afforded the ranch when he'd purchased it. In the dark, she navigated the road as if she'd driven it as many times as the road from Huckleberry to her ranch. Her lights caught on the pole gate and fence denoting the beginning of the Higheagle property. It sounded like Coop planned to live elsewhere when he received his degree. What about Andy? Would he stay on to keep the Higheagle Ranch in the family?

She parked where she had the night before. Turning off the engine, she sat a minute in the Jeep. It would be terrible if the ranch didn't stay in the Higheagle family. Her father and Aunt Jo were the only children of Minnie and Joseph. Maybe one of Velma's children would be interested, though they weren't Higheagles they were family.

The light at the back door came on. Aunt Jo stuck her head out. Shandra exited the Jeep and walked to the house.

"I thought you pulled in, but when you didn't come in, I thought maybe I didn't hear right." Jo held the door wide open, allowing the comforting aroma of baked bread and fried meat to swirl around her head.

"Dinner smells delicious. Will it be just us?" she asked, hoping for some time with this family without being pulled by other family members.

"It will be you, me, Martin, and Andy. Coop called to say he was going to Alexander's house after practice and he'd bring him home." Jo closed the doors and moved to the stove.

"I'll put my things in my room and come back down to help." Shandra headed to the door out of the kitchen.

"I don't need any help, but you can visit while I finish up." Jo smiled and busied herself at the stove.

Shandra hurried up the stairs, deposited her things

on the bed, and returned to the kitchen.

"How did Charlie behave?" Jo asked, without any preamble.

"Like a man who is losing sight of reality. His house is a hovel. Beer cans, magazines and newspapers, and half eaten TV dinners are all over. There are even mice in his house." Shandra was still trying to make sense of a man who had once been driven to be so uncaring of everything around him.

Jo shook her head. "You'd be surprised how many homes on the reservation you'll find like that. If they don't see hope, they lose track of life."

"Are there any in this family like that?" Shandra hadn't noticed anyone the night before who looked despondent.

"There are some. We try to keep them included and help them on their bad days." Jo's eyes appeared misty.

It was evident she held family dear.

"Were any at the dinner last night?" Shandra wanted to reach out to them. See if she could discover how to help.

"No. The more you visit they will come to see you as family and not a busybody." Jo handed Shandra plates. "Tell me about Charlie."

Shandra recounted her conversation.

"You didn't ask him how he could afford the ranch?" Aunt Jo asked, handing Shandra the eating utensils.

"No. How would one go about discovering how he came into possession of that land?"

"I would imagine you'd find the records in the agency offices somewhere."

Stomping at the back door turned their attention to Martin and Andy entering the kitchen.

They were both bundled up. As they took off their stocking caps and coats, bits of hay drifted to the floor.

"Looks like you two were doing the chores," Shandra said, grabbing the broom by the door and sweeping the hay into a small pile.

"The livestock on this place takes time to feed and check on," Martin said, sitting on the bench by the back door and unlacing his boots.

"Do you still breed horses?" Shandra hadn't had time to ask all the questions that had bounced around in her head on the drive to the reservation.

"Yes, only now we are breeding purebred appaloosas." The enthusiasm in Andy's voice made Shandra happy.

"I take it you're a horseman like my father?" she asked.

"Not really. I like the vet part of animals. Keeping them healthy, seeing how breeding makes a better animal." Andy's eyes danced with excitement.

"I'm so glad someone will be interested in keeping this ranch in the family." She hugged Andy. Surprising both him and herself.

Jo laughed. "We've been worried you would want the ranch."

Shandra looked each one in the eyes. "No. I have a beautiful ranch on Huckleberry Mountain. You're all welcome to come visit any time. It felt like home the minute I set foot on the property. But I was worried no one would want to stay on here and preserve great-grandfather's legacy."

"Coop has never shown any interest in the land or animals. But Andy. He's been hugging animals since he was big enough to crawl over to our old dog." Martin ruffled his son's hair. The teenager smashed it back down and narrowed his eyes at his father.

"I'm happy to know it will be in good hands. And I'd like to purchase an appaloosa or two from you. I have one. His name is Apple."

They all laughed and sat at the table. Jo had placed dishes of food on the table as they talked.

Halfway through the meal, Shandra heard a jazz tune playing. "My phone." She jumped up from the table and raced up the stairs. The music had stopped by the time she pulled the phone out of her purse. She looked at the call back number but didn't know who it was.

Carrying the phone downstairs, she realized it was a local number. She checked the voice mail. No messages.

Why would someone try to call her and not leave a message?

"Do you know who this number belongs to?" Shandra handed her phone around the table.

"It's local," both Jo and Martin said.

"Call it back," Andy said, with the logical idea.

Shandra smiled at him. "That would be the best way to figure it out." She punched in redial.

Two rings and a gruff voice said, "Ketch Pen."

Shandra peered at the people around the table. "It's the Ketch Pen?"

"Ask for Coop," Andy said.

"Is Coop Elwood there, please," Shandra asked.

The man laughed. "Is this a joke? No one asks for Coop that nice."

"Gimme that!" Coop's voice mumbled in the background.

"Shandra?" he asked.

"Yes. Why did you call me? How did you get my number?" She didn't remember giving him her number.

"I'll tell you later. Come down here with Dad. There's someone here who knows a lot about Charlie Frank, and she is willing to tell anyone who buys her a drink."

Shandra cast a glance at Martin. "Who is it?"

"Jessie Lawyer."

The name didn't mean anything to Shandra. "I'll tell your dad and we'll meet you there."

"What was that?" Jo asked.

"That was Coop. He wants Martin and I to meet him at the Ketch Pen to talk to Jessie Lawyer."

Aunt Jo's eyes widened and her mouth puckered. "I don't want either of you talking to Jessie."

Shandra didn't know why Jo was so adamant. "Coop said she has a lot to say about Charlie Frank."

Jo's eyes flashed to her husband. "She has a lot to say about a lot of men."

Martin's face darkened in color. "Jo that was a long time ago. Before you stole my heart."

"I don't trust her!" Jo crossed her arms. "I don't want either of you going there. Andy go get your brother."

"Aunt Jo. If she knows something I have to talk to her. I'll go by myself." Shandra picked up her dishes and placed them in the sink.

"No. It's best to have someone with you. I'll call Velma. Pick her up before you go to the tavern." Jo moved to the phone.

Shandra didn't know why Aunt Jo was so adamant about taking someone with her, and not her husband, but she'd take the dog if that made Jo happy and got Shandra a chance to visit with this Jessie person. She gathered her coat and purse and headed out into the night. She'd planned on a nice evening catching up on the whole family, not walking into a tavern on the reservation.

Chapter Ten

Shandra picked up Velma. She was standing in the front window waiting for her. As they drove the short distance to the tavern, Shandra asked the question that had been on her mind since starting up the Jeep and heading back to Nespelem. "Why is Jo so against Jessie Lawyer?"

Velma stared out the front window of the vehicle. "Jessie isn't Indian. She worked the rodeo circuit back when Edward, Charlie, and Martin were rodeoing."

"Martin? I didn't know he rodeoed." Another fact she would stick away.

"He was several years behind the other two. It was his first year on the circuit. Edward tried to keep an eye on him. He knew Jo had her heart set on Martin. Jessie got drunk one night and flirted with Martin. She sent him all kind of female signals. And like any man that age, he fell for the signals. Only when he acted on what he thought she wanted, she started hollering rape. I don't know what she thought she'd get out of the whole spectacle. All it did was hurt Martin's family and Jo has never forgiven Jessie."

"If she isn't Indian what is she doing drinking in a reservation tavern?" Shandra was pretty sure only reservation residents hung out in the tavern.

"She married Raymond Lawyer after living with Charlie Frank for about five years. Ten years after her marriage to Raymond, she started drinking heavy." Velma glanced over at Shandra. "Be careful of her. She may be drunk, but she's still very much like the coyote."

A square wooden building with a lighted Ketch Pen sign came into view.

Shandra pulled up alongside a beat up Ford and parked. "You don't have to go in," she said to Velma.

"You need someone to be there to make sure she doesn't play tricks with you. That is why Coop asked for his father. He doesn't know the story behind Martin and Jessie. But he does know Jessie's antics." Velma slid out of the Jeep and led the way into the Ketch Pen.

Shandra stepped through the door and was surrounded by heat, the odor of stale beer, and murky lighting. The lights over the pool tables beamed down like beacons onto the green felt surface and backs of the heads of the people leaning over the tables. A half dozen locals wielded pool cues. The crack of balls hitting punctuated the murmuring of the people at the scattered tables and bar.

Velma tapped Shandra on the shoulder and pointed

to a wall. An array of photographs hung on the wall. Walking along, squinting at each photo depicting a Native American either in a race car or other sporting event, her heart stopped when she spotted a photo of Edward Higheagle. He held up a belt buckle and had a huge grin on his face. She reached out, touching her father's face under the cold, grimy glass of the picture frame.

Velma cleared her throat, reminding Shandra why they were here. She tore her gaze away from her father and headed to a table.

Coop moved away from the bar and headed straight to them. "Why'd you bring Aunt?" he asked.

Shandra glanced at Velma.

"Because your mom had chores for your dad," Velma said, nodding her head toward an average-sized woman with a tight, pink, long-sleeved shirt that had sparkles cascading down the front. The fabric stretched over her middle making a pretty pink muffin top. The dim lights made it hard to tell if her hair was bleached blonde or silver. It was in a style of the nineteen-seventies. Hair spray plastered bangs that rose from her forehead and swooped over the top of her head like photos of the Nez Perce men in the 1800s. The longer locks were pulled up into a fluffy ponytail tied with a pink ribbon.

"That's Jessie?" Shandra asked.

Velma and Coop nodded.

"Do you suggest I introduce myself or just sit down and start up a conversation?" She didn't have a clue how to approach this woman who had a history with both her family and Charlie Frank.

"Don't tell her you're a Higheagle," Velma advised.

Shandra rolled her eyes. Great. She had to figure out how to bring this woman into a conversation about thirty years ago and not tell her who she was and why she wanted to know. Glancing around the room, she spotted a poster for the Omak Stampede. It was worth a try.

She slung her bag over her shoulder and sat down on the bar stool next to Jessie. The woman looked her up and down, staring a long time at Shandra's four-hundred-dollar boots.

"Nice boots," Jessie said.

"Thanks. It took a while to save the money to get them." Shandra glanced at Jessie's feet. She wore cowboy boots too. Not as expensive but a good brand. So she liked boots. "Yours are nice. But you look like a real cowgirl. Your boots have been worn for more than walking around."

Jessie smiled at her. Her teeth didn't shine in the bar lights. They were brown squares that looked stained from tobacco smoke. "I was a rodeo queen years ago, tried the barrel circuit, then just stuck to training horses."

"Really? You train barrel horses? I've always wondered what it took to train a horse to go fast around the barrels." Shandra felt someone take the seat next to her. She glanced sideways. It was Coop. He ordered a beer. She glanced around the room and found Velma at the table closest to them with her chair turned to keep an ear on the conversation.

Jessie took a long draw on her beer and turned her

attention to Shandra. "Why do you want to know about barrel racing?"

"Curiosity I guess."

The older woman took another draw on the beer and fingered an unlit cigarette laying on the counter. She wanted to smoke. "You really interested in barrel racing?" Jessie asked.

Shandra nodded.

"You want the horse to learn to bend their ribcage, making their body in the shape of a 'C' this…."

Shandra stared at the woman talking, but her mind mixed and re-mixed what she knew about this woman and how to get her to talk about Charlie Frank.

"And that's how you train a horse to run the barrels," Jessie said.

"That's fascinating. I've heard of another person who lives on the reservation who trains horses." Shandra tapped her chin as if thinking. "I think it's race horses."

"There's Randy Holmes. Wolf Red Cloud."

"No, that doesn't sound right. He's been around a while. Charlie. Charlie something."

Jessie coughed, fiddled with the cigarette, rolling it back and forth on the bar, and said, "Charlie Frank."

"That's it. He had two first names." Shandra smiled at Jessie.

She narrowed her eyes. "Why would you want to know about that deadbeat?"

"His name came up in a conversation I had with Phil Seeton. I think they used to rodeo together or something." If she couldn't use her father, she'd use Phil. She was pretty sure he wouldn't mind. "He told me about Charlie having a ranch and training horses."

"Where did you run into Phil Seeton? He was nothing but a drunk. He couldn't sit a horse to save his soul." Jessie lifted her glass for a refill.

When the bartender put it down, Shandra pulled out her wallet. "I'll get this, and I'll have whatever you have on tap."

"We don't have tap. It comes out of a bottle," the bartender said.

"I'll have something out of a bottle then. But poured in a glass." Shandra didn't know the names of beer. She was a wine drinker, but had a feeling ordering wine in here would get her thrown out.

The bartender slid a glass of beer her way.

"Thanks. What's your name?" Jessie tipped her glass to Shandra in a salute and took a long drink.

"Ann." It was her middle name. She never used it, but this seemed like as good a time as any. Shandra was uncommon.

"Ann, did Phil tell you he made a better announcer once he sobered up than he did a rider?" Jessie let loose a crackly, smoker's cackle at her own humor.

"No. He told me how he sobered up and how he wasn't as prejudice against Indian rodeo contestants as some of the others back then." She sipped her beer. "Is that true? Was he kind to the Native American riders? Were they hassled a lot?"

Jessie picked up the unlit cigarette as if to puff on it, then set it back on the bar and turned to her. "Why are you asking all these questions that sound like you're a do-gooder?"

"I'm writing a paper on the inequalities of rodeo to

the ethnic groups. I'm starting in the past and working my way forward." Shandra wasn't sure if she liked that she could think so fast or that she was becoming too good of a liar.

"You're doing a paper on the inequalities of ethnic groups in rodeo? What about women? We took a backseat to the guys for years. Still do in some ways." She gulped the last half of her beer and smacked the bottle on the bar.

Shandra motioned for the bartender to give Jessie another one.

"That was what I wanted to do my paper on and my professor was against it." That was one of the more truthful things she'd said about this make-believe story. Her professor when she was in college would have had nothing to do with a thesis that would have extolled how women were poorly treated in a profession. He was the most chauvinistic, possessive man she'd ever had the poor judgement to get tangled with.

Jessie nodded. "Bet he's a man."

Shandra smiled at the fact Jessie was getting a bit loose and could hopefully give her an earful. "Yes, he is a man."

"You want to know how the Indian boys were treated by the rodeo association?" Jessie asked, taking a couple more swallows of her beer.

"Yes, I would." Shandra watched the woman closely.

"Where's your notepad and pen?" Jessie asked, narrowing her eyes.

Shandra pulled her phone out of her purse. "I tape everything. Is that okay with you?"

Jessie eyed the phone suspiciously. "That got one of them recorder apps on it?"

"Yes." Shandra put her finger on the side as if she were pressing a button. "Please state your name and that you don't mind answering my questions."

The bartender leaned on the bar. "What's going on here?"

Shandra looked the man square in the eyes and lied. "I'm doing a thesis on the inequalities the Native American cowboy suffered from the rodeo association."

The man stared at her a minute more, then rubbed a towel on the counter. "Jessie should know, she's slept with all of them."

"That's not true," she slurred.

"That's right. Edward was the only one who wouldn't slip into the gutter with you." The bartender moved off before Jessie could retort.

Shandra's interest went on high alert at the mention of Edward. She didn't think there were many Native American Edwards from this area who rodeoed.

"Damn him. He always stuck his nose in the air at me, then rooted around with that snooty White princess and ended up catching her by getting her pregnant." Jessie guzzled the rest of her drink. "Gotta pee." She picked up her cigarette and slid off the bar stool, weaving her way to the ladies room.

Shandra slipped off the stool and walked over to Velma. "Will she be back?"

"I don't think she leaves here until she's thrown out or Raymond comes and gets her," Velma said. "That's what I've heard."

Coop grabbed Shandra's arm. "She's coming

back."

Shandra slid back on her bar stool and sipped her drink. A jazz tune jingled from her phone. She glanced at the name and hit ignore. Then quickly typed. *Call you back soon.*

"What are you doin'?" Jessie asked, kind of oozing back onto the bar stool. She picked up her empty glass and stared at Shandra.

Getting someone drunk to get information and then sending them out to possibly drive a vehicle wasn't something Shandra felt she could deal with. Coop bumped her arm. She glanced at him and he raised his beer.

"I was texting my friend. Letting him know I'd call him later." Shandra waved her hand to the bartender. He grinned. She'd bet it wasn't often he got money from an off reservation patron.

"What's his name?" Jessie asked.

"Who?" Shandra asked to stall.

"Your boyfriend." Jessie picked up the bottle the bartender brought over and took two big swallows.

For a small woman she could sure down a lot of beer.

"Ryan."

"He a cowboy?" Jessie asked, her dull grey eyes glinting with interest.

"Not for a living." She had to change the subject soon or she'd ask his occupation. "You were going to tell me about Charlie, Phil, and someone named Edward?" Shandra took a chance that would get the woman chatty again.

"I don't want to talk about Edward!" she shouted

and shoved the bottle of beer across the bar and onto the floor behind the bar.

Chapter Eleven

The bartender hurried over, glaring at Shandra. "What are you doing upsetting my customers?"

"I didn't mean to. I just asked her a question about the men she knew from here that rodeoed."

A couple of the men who were playing pool walked up to the bar, their pool cues in their hands. "Someone bothering you, Jessie?" the oldest one asked.

"I'm not bothering her... I..."

Coop grabbed her arm. "We were leaving."

"Ain't you Martin Elwood's oldest?" the younger man asked.

"Elwood?" Jessie came off the stool with her claws out.

Shandra shoved Coop behind her. The drunk woman came at her, but slammed against the bar when Velma shoved her from the side.

"We don't want no trouble with you, Roger." Velma shooed Coop and Shandra toward the door.

The older man was helping Jessie off the floor when Shandra turned her back on the bar and shoved out into the brisk night air.

"I learned nothing!" Shandra said in frustration.

Velma climbed into the passenger seat and Coop the back seat of the Jeep.

Shandra started the engine and backed out. She hadn't found out a thing other than she could lie when the instance called for it.

Velma patted her arm. "Jo would be proud of the way you protected her boy."

"I didn't need protecting," Coop said dejectedly from the back seat.

"I'm pretty sure Jessie won't talk to me again any time soon. I never learned anything about Charlie." Shandra made up her mind to look for answers in the rodeo association and the people who were at the rodeo the day her father died. She could get a list of the contestants and start interviewing them. Someone had to have seen something.

She pulled into Velma's driveway. Lights blazed out of every window and music played loudly.

Velma had her door open and her foot out on the ground before Shandra put on the brake.

"Go on home. I'll handle this." Velma charged up to her door.

"Lawrence is going to be in trouble," Coop said, sliding into the seat his aunt vacated.

"Who's Lawrence?" Shandra asked backing out the drive. Young men and women started flowing out of

Velma's house.

"Velma's youngest. He holds a party every time his mom is out for the evening." Coop laughed. "He gets yelled at and Velma threatens to throw him out of the house and he's there the next day."

"Poor Velma." Shandra knew she should call Ryan but didn't want to with Coop listening in. Once they arrived at the ranch, she motioned to Coop. "Go on in. I'll be there in a minute. I need to call Ryan."

Coop slid out the door and walked into the house.

Shandra kept the Jeep running to stay warm and dialed Ryan.

"What took you so long to call back?" Ryan asked.

"Hello to you," Shandra said. She'd known he'd be worried, but she hadn't expected him to voice his concern so quickly.

"Sorry. I couldn't figure out why you'd text me and not pick up the call."

The contriteness in his voice soften her attitude. "I was in a bar and later in an almost bar fight."

"See, I did have reason to be worried. Who did you almost get in a fight with?" His joking tone made her smile.

"A drunk woman who tried to sleep with my father."

"What?"

Shandra laughed. "Yeah, it seems every White woman on the rodeo circuit thirty years ago wanted to sleep with my father. I'm not sure if I should be proud or disgusted."

Ryan laughed. "You still coming tomorrow?"

"Yes. Trying to get information around here is like

getting swallowed up in a tornado. Only little bits and pieces get spit out and I can't make any sense of them."

"I made sure no one calls me in to work tomorrow. Maybe we can piece some of the bits together."

Shandra smiled. "I'd like that.

"See you about ten?" Ryan asked.

"Yes. Good-night."

"Night."

Shandra hung up, turned the Jeep off, and headed into the house.

"And then Jessie came at me like a wild cat, claws bared and screeching—"

Shandra cut Coop off. "And I shoved him behind me and Velma pushed Jessie into the bar."

Jo and Andy's wide eyes said they hadn't come up against Jessie when she was drunk. Martin shook his head.

"You just ruined my story," Coop moaned.

Everyone laughed at his dejected stance and expression.

"Did you learn anything?" Jo asked.

"Not really. I'll go home and see if I can dig up some information from other people who were at the rodeo the day father died." Shandra continued through the kitchen. "I'm turning in."

"Good night," chorused the family in the kitchen.

"Good night." Shandra climbed the stairs, got ready for bed, and climbed in. Her mind raced with the events at the bar. Eventually, she slipped off to sleep.

Ella stood by Shandra's bed, moving her hands in a way that swirled the air. Heads popped out of a small tornado. Charlie Frank. Jessie Lawyer. Father. Mother.

Adam. And a man she didn't know. The air moved faster and faster. The heads popped in and out mixing faces, changing expressions.

"Stop. Stop," mumbled Shandra.

The faces blurred, the air swirled, and turned into the horses, standing in a circle, looking down at Father.

"No!" Shandra shouted and sat upright in bed.

Footsteps pounded down the hall and her door swung open. Coop stood in the door with a bat in his hand. Andy peered around him.

"You okay, Shandra?" Coop asked.

"Yes. Sorry. It was a nightmare. Go back to bed." She shoved her fingers through her hair, shoving it off her face. It had tangled around her head like a web.

"You sure?" Coop set the bat on his shoulder.

"Yeah. Go back to bed." She waited until the two closed the door and she heard their footsteps retreating, before she turned on the light. Picking up her tablet, she started the hunt for the people at the rodeo the day of her father's death. She wanted to know who the man was in her dream.

***

Ryan paced from his living room into the kitchen. Shandra had called this morning saying she'd slept in and wouldn't get there until noon. She wouldn't say why she'd slept in, but he had a hunch she'd had a dream that included her grandmother. If the other police in the department knew he believed in her dreams they'd release him on grounds of insanity. However, his childhood had been full of tales of wee people and the like from his Irish mother. She'd told enough stories that he didn't doubt Shandra's grandmother came to her

86

in dreams. What he didn't like was not knowing if a dream would put Shandra in danger.

The sound of a car pulling up to his house, catapulted him to the front door. Shandra climbed out of her Jeep, hugging her coat tighter to her.

"Come in and get warmed up before I take you to lunch." Ryan held out a hand.

She wrapped her fingers around his in a tight grip.

"What's wrong?" he asked, leading her through the door and hugging her to him.

"There was a nasty wreck about twenty minutes out of Warner." She wrapped her arms around him. "If I hadn't slept in, I could have been caught in it."

Ryan hugged her close and kissed the top of her head. He'd missed her and worried about her, but his thoughts hadn't gone to the possibility she was in danger from the snowfall they'd had the night before.

"We can sit and talk before going to lunch." Ryan released her, slipping her coat from her shoulders.

"I'd like that. And maybe a cup of something hot, not coffee." Her gaze fell on his velvet painting of dogs playing cards. "I can't believe you still have that hanging there."

"I haven't found anything to replace it and it's better than a large blank wall." He tossed her coat over the back of his recliner and headed to the kitchen. "I have the tea you like."

He heard her boot heels clicking behind him.

"How do you know what tea I like?" She stopped at the kitchen table and took a seat.

"I've spent enough time at your house to use my skills as a detective to discover your favorite things."

Ryan had the kettle already heated. He poured water into a cup with a green and white tea mix in a tea thing. There was a name for the little ball with millions of holes, but all he had to do was walk into the store ask for the section that had tea items and pick it up.

He carried the cup still steeping over to Shandra along with a small plate, spoon, and jar of honey.

"You do seem to know me," Shandra said, sniffing the steam and tapping the honey with her finger.

Ryan poured a cup of coffee and took the seat across the table from Shandra. "Tell me about your trip."

As Shandra told him about all the missed opportunities to gather information, he felt her frustration. "You don't know how this Charlie came to afford a ranch after your father's death. And you find this woman, Jessie's, comment about your father and mother upsetting."

"I feel like the trip didn't give me answers, only more questions. And then my dream last night. Heads of all the people involved with Father back then and one I didn't recognize. Until hours later." She took a sip of the tea.

"What do you mean hours later? Did your grandmother come to your dreams twice last night?" He'd wondered if by going to her grandmother's house, Shandra would feel her grandmother's presence more.

"No. After the dream I searched the internet and discovered the man I didn't know is Dicky Harmond. He was a rodeo clown when Father, Charlie, and Phil were participating in rodeos. And he worked the same circuit." Shandra frowned. "But I couldn't find much about him after that season ended."

"Where did he live?" Ryan could put out some feelers, see if the man was still alive.

"In Oregon." Shandra shook her head. "From what I could tell he moved around a lot."

"I'll see if I can find him." Ryan held his hand out across the table. Shandra placed her palm against his. "You knew when you started this, it would be hard to find answers. Don't let it consume you to the point you can't do your art."

A faint smile tipped the corners of her lips. "I understand your concern, but knowing the truth about why my father was taken from me…it isn't an obsession, it's a need to know the truth. It will help me move forward." She squeezed his hand. "It will help me understand what I need from life."

Ryan nodded. He'd realized from his first meeting with Shandra there was something in her past that held her back from committing to a relationship. Perhaps this hunt for the truth about her father would bring them closer.

"Finish your tea. I want to take you to a new café I found." His mom had been after him to invite Shandra to the ranch for Christmas. But after the remarks made by his father at Conor and Lissa's wedding, he didn't plan on taking her around his family any time soon. But he was hoping for an invite to her ranch for Christmas. It was only three weeks away.

Shandra drank the rest of her tea, used his bathroom, and they walked toward the city center.

"Why are we walking?" Shandra asked. "Not that I mind."

"I wanted to show you the charm of this town." Ryan gently squeezed Shandra's hand, tucked into his. "They have the Christmas decorations up. With the snow, it looks like a scene out of a Christmas movie."

Chapter Twelve

Shandra enjoyed her lunch with Ryan and the stroll they took through Warner, window shopping and wandering through some of the shops to get warm and make purchases. She wanted to ask him to spend Christmas with her, but knew he had obligations to spend the day with his family. And given the way his father behaved at Conor's wedding, she didn't think she wanted to spend a day with his family. Not until she was certain about Ryan fitting into her future.

Climbing into her Jeep, Shandra reached to close the door.

Ryan held onto the door. "When will I see or hear from you again?"

Shandra shrugged. "When you learn more about the rodeo clown or I discover something. Why?"

"That's not a concrete answer." He released the

door and moved to her side. "I have two days off starting Monday. Would you like some company for a couple of days?"

She knew he was asking if he could stay at the ranch. The idea of sitting in front of a fire and watching the snow fall outside with Ryan on the couch beside her was inviting. "Yes, you may visit."

"I could help you get a Christmas tree." Ryan's eyes lit up.

Shandra laughed.

"I could."

"You look like a young boy anxious for Christmas." She liked this carefree Ryan. He was always on alert.

"Could be this year it looks a lot more promising than the last few years." His youthful glow heated into desire.

She knew what he wanted for Christmas. Her head wasn't ready to become that attached to a man just yet. "You know we don't always get what we wish for."

His expression didn't change. "There's a difference between wishing and knowing it is inevitable." He leaned in, kissed her, and then backed away. "See you Monday." He closed the door and watched her.

Shandra started the Jeep. She glanced Ryan's direction. He held up his hand miming to call. She knew he meant when she arrived home safe. Nodding, she backed out of his drive and headed home as the sun dropped from sight, filling the dark satin sky with sparkling stars.

The drive home took twice as long as normal due to the slick roads. Heading up her drive, she was thankful that Lil was so tenacious. The snow had been cleared leaving a much smoother ride with the snow filling in the pot holes in her dirt drive.

The twinkling of lights, like the stars only down low, caught her attention and when she drove into the meadow in front of the house and barn, she was delighted to see strings of white Christmas lights across the front of the house, the studio, and the barn. There was just the right amount to look festive and not gaudy.

She pulled up to the barn. The doors opened. Sheba bounded out, her tongue lolling to one side. She stood on her back legs and put her paws on the window, looking in at Shandra.

"Come on, Sheba, let her park the Jeep!" Lil called, waiting by the barn door.

Sheba dropped to all fours and trotted to Lil.

Shandra drove the Jeep into the area she used in the wintertime to keep the Jeep out of the weather. As soon as she opened the door, a big furry, black head shoved into her lap.

"I missed you too." Shandra rubbed her cheek across the top of Sheba's head and kissed her. "Help me get my stuff unloaded." She shoved the dog backwards gently and slid out of the seat.

Lil already had the back door open, lifting out Shandra's bag and the bag of items she'd purchased in Warner with Ryan.

"Looks like you did some shopping." Lil handed the bags to Shandra. "The fireplace is going and I put a crock of soup on."

Shandra hugged Lil. "Thank you! I'm starving but wasn't in the mood to figure out what to eat."

Lil ducked out of the embrace. "You're welcome. Go on. I'll get the doors."

Shandra called to Sheba, and they made their way to the back door of the house. Her phone rang as she set her bag of clothes on the chair and the shopping bag on the table. To Shandra's surprise, it was her mother.

"Hello?" she answered wondering why her mother would be calling. They didn't talk on a regular basis. In fact, they usually only called each other when they needed something.

"Shandra, this is your mother." Celeste said that every time, as if Shandra wouldn't see it on her phone or recognize her voice.

"I know. Why are you calling me? Aren't you at the National Finals Rodeo in Las Vegas?" She was ashamed the question came out sounding a bit on the snotty side. But since leaving home after high school graduation, her mother only remembered she had a daughter when she could use Shandra's reputation to her advantage.

"Yes. We're at the Finals. I'm calling you for Adam."

Shandra rolled her eyes. What could her stepfather want? But then she had asked them some questions about the rodeo a while back. This was his way of collecting for giving her the answers she wanted. "What does Adam want?"

"We learned that there are two new Committee Chairs in the circuit Adam provides rough stock for. To get to know them better we decided to host a holiday dinner party for the members of the rodeo associations in Montana that Adam works closest with. He'd like you to attend."

That her mother said Adam would like her to attend made Shandra wonder if her mother would like her to be there as well.

"When is this dinner party? And can I bring a guest?" Shandra knew that would pique her mother's attention.

"Not that awful woman who helps you, I hope." Celeste's tone alone made Shandra want to decline, but it was the rodeo association. The people she wanted to talk to. Most would be the right age to remember her father and possibly the day of the accident.

"No, she wouldn't attend. I'd like to bring Ryan Greer."

"Wonderful! What does he do?"

"He's a detective with the Weippe County Sheriff's Office."

"Not the man who was going to arrest you!"

Shandra smiled. "He didn't arrest me. When is the dinner?"

"A week from this coming Saturday. Seven. I'll have a room ready for you and Ryan."

"We won't be spending the night," Shandra said. There was no way she'd spend the night at Adam's house.

"But you can't drive home after the dinner party, they usually last till eleven, some even later." Her mother didn't sound worried about her daughter more about what people would think if Shandra left early.

"We'll leave when we're ready. Why does Adam want me there?" Shandra knew there had to be a catch.

"One of the new committee members, the one who

will contract the rough stock, likes Native American art. Adam thought you could talk about that with Wes Pickley." Her mother's voice was muffled for a moment. "I have to go. They're getting ready for the bareback riding."

The sound of the crowd came through. Why didn't I notice it before?

"I'll tell Adam you'll be coming?" her mother questioned as if making sure Shandra wouldn't back out.

"Ryan and I will be there." Shandra tapped the off button.

Sheba shoved her head under Shandra's empty hand.

"I know, you want your lovin's. Just one more call." She scratched Sheba's ears. "Go wait for me by the fire and I'll bring you a treat."

The black ears lifted and Sheba's tongue lolled out of her mouth. She padded on her large paws into the living room.

Shandra slipped her phone into her back pocket and scooped a bowl of creamy potato soup, placed it on a plate with two slices of sour dough French bread, well-buttered. She poured a glass of wine and carried the food and beverage into the couch. After placing the dishes on the table, she pulled out her phone and dialed Ryan.

"Hello," he answered after two rings.

"You answered so fast I'd think you were waiting for me to call," she teased, placing the plate and soup on her lap.

"I was. How were the roads? According to Ron

there were a lot of accidents all around the county today."

"The road between Warner and Huckleberry was plowed pretty good. There is already a lot of traffic headed to the Huckleberry ski area. Those are the people I worry about. In a hurry to get an extra fifteen minutes of skiing in." Shandra had two vehicles full of what looked to be college kids pass her as if she were standing still. She was certain she'd see them in a snow bank but luck was with them. She never did see the back end of either car.

"I'm glad you made it home safe," Ryan said.

"I had a call as soon as I arrived." She was certain if Ryan could get off he'd go to the party with her, but taking him to the place she grew up made it look like she was wanting him to get to know her family.

"Was it about your recent trip?" His business-like tone made her smile.

"No. It was my mother."

"Isn't she and your stepfather in Las Vegas at the National Finals?"

The suspicion in his voice revealed he had the same perception of her parents as she did.

"They are. Adam learned of some new committee members in his circuit and has planned a dinner party a week from this Saturday after they get back." She waited. He'd pick up the bait she'd dangled.

"A dinner party. Were you invited?"

"Yes. It's with people in the rodeo industry. If you don't dig something up about Harmond and I can't get more on Charlie Frank and Jessie, then we'll have a room full of people to visit with."

"Did I hear you say 'we'. As in, I've been invited too?" Ryan's tone became suspicious again.

"You weren't invited by my mom, I said I was bringing a guest. I thought I should let you know before I see you on Monday. It would give you more time to see if you can get that Saturday off." She knew he would make sure he could go, but she held her breath. Would he put more into it than she wanted?

"The only thing that would keep me from going to that party with you would be the weather." His voice deepened with pleasure.

"Thank you. Two of us asking questions will get more information gathered in one night than if I went alone." She'd wait until just before the party and ask her mother for all the names of the attendees.

"That's the only reason you're inviting me? To help interrogate people?"

Shandra stirred the soup sitting in her lap. "That and to keep me company."

"That I can do. We can discuss more when I see you Monday."

"I agree. Good night."

"Night."

Shandra tapped the off button and tossed the phone to the other side of the couch. She peeled the crust from one of the slices of bread and dangled it in the air. Sheba slowly rose from her spot at Shandra's feet and opened her mouth. Shandra tossed the crust into the dog's mouth.

Eating her soup and tossing more of her bread to Sheba than she ate herself, Shandra stared at her computer. Aunt Jo had given her Jessie's maiden name that morning before Shandra left. It would be the name most of the rodeo participants would know the ex-barrel racer by. With her dinner finished, Shandra set the plate and bowl to the side and slid her laptop to the edge of the coffee table.

Sipping her wine, Shandra typed one-handed, putting Jessie Preston into the search engine. To her surprise there was a lot about the woman. A video on barrel racing, a place to sign up for a class given by Jessie Preston-Lawyer, and a photo of Jessie back in the eighties when she was competing.

Shandra zoomed the photo in. It was a bit grainy, but she was positive the man standing behind Jessie, and looking as pleased as the barrel racer with her check, was Dicky Harmond. That couldn't be a coincidence that he was standing in a possessive way behind her. Now that she had more names, seeing Phil Seeton was next, while Ryan dug up what he could on Dicky Harmond.

Chapter Thirteen

Shandra pulled the vase out of the kiln early the following morning. The crackle look she'd hoped for on the glaze had turned out. She had time to try this on a couple more pieces before the February show and then she could do a tutorial on it in New Mexico.

Stomping outside the back door of the studio meant Lil was done with the morning chores. The door opened, blowing in cold air along with the eccentric woman in purple insulated overalls and her usual purple coat and stocking cap.

"Where's Lewis?" Shandra asked, seeing a purple and lime green knitted scarf around Lil's neck instead of yellow fur.

"He thought it was too cold to come out." Lil pulled off her thermal gloves and nodded to the buckets of clay they'd cleaned and stored so Shandra would have clay to work with through the winter while the clay pockets were covered with snow. "You going to work on something today?"

Lil was better than a conscience. She said out loud what bounced around inside Shandra's head.

"Not today. I'm heading to Missoula to visit with Phil Seeton. You want to come along? You two do know one another."

"Someone needs to stay here for the animals in case you get stuck over there. There is another snow storm coming through." Lil eyed her. "Why you need to visit with Phil again?"

"I have a couple more names that seem to be connected to my father. Dicky Harmond and Jessie Preston."

Lil cringed at both names. "I didn't realize your daddy hung around with the likes of them."

"You were at some of the rodeos with Johnny that Father participated in. What can you tell me about Jessie and Dicky?" Shandra walked over and sat in the padded chair she sometimes sat in while drawing her next project.

Lil grabbed a folding chair sitting at the table where they glazed and sat in front of Shandra. She pulled her stocking cap off, making her short white hair spark and wave with static electricity.

"Johnny once told me Jessie liked Indian cowboys. But I don't think she ever dated your daddy. No, I'm pretty sure she didn't. I remember her shoving your mom at a rodeo. I don't know what the conversation was, but Jessie was angry and your mom looked upset. That was a rodeo or two before your daddy's accident."

Lil leaned forward, her gaze on her worn cowboy boots. "Dicky was mean. He was an average-sized man but thought he was bigger and tougher. If he didn't like something the girl he was dating did, he'd knock her around. I heard your daddy stopped him from beating a girl in a parking lot. It drew a crowd and Dicky always made Indian comments after that when your daddy was around." She shook her head. "He was mean even when he wasn't drunk. But drunk…Johnny told me he threatened a cowboy at a party and the next rodeo that cowboy was injured real bad. But no one could point a finger at Dicky."

A shiver ran down Shandra's back. Dicky would be in his sixties now, possibly seventies depending on his age at that time. He wasn't a physical threat that she could think of but hearing about him, he was her first clear suspect in her father's death.

"If you think of anything else, call me or tell me when I get back. I should be back by late afternoon figuring in three hours for the weather." Shandra stood. "I'll take Sheba with me. Maybe I can talk the people at the nursing home into letting her come in and visit Phil."

"He's gonna think you're bringing in a miniature pony," Lil quipped.

Shandra laughed. "Could be. See you this evening."

***

Shandra shared the fries she bought at a drive-through with Sheba while sitting in the Jeep in the nursing home parking lot. The drive had taken even longer than usual. A semi-truck had jack-knifed, causing a backup on both sides of the interstate. She ate all the cardboard hamburger she could stomach and gave the rest to Sheba. She downed it in one bite and snuffled Shandra's shoulder looking for more.

"Ready to be a therapy dog?" Shandra asked her companion.

She climbed out of the Jeep and opened the passenger door. "Whoa! You have to be properly suited up." So people wouldn't worry about Sheba's size, Shandra put a harness on her. With the harness in place, Sheba jumped out of the vehicle.

"Wait a minute, you need your buddy." Shandra slipped the legs of a stuffed monkey, wearing a cowboy hat, into the loops on the harness that made the toy look like it was riding Sheba. It had been Lil's idea to make the huge dog look approachable. Whenever Shandra took Sheba to public events or places, Shandra put the harness and monkey on the dog.

"Let's go." Shandra shouldered her bag, shut the doors on the Jeep, and locked it.

They encountered a bit of resistance at the front door of the nursing home. Once the residents crowded around, and Sheba licked and talked to everyone, the nurses decided she could enter the premises.

"Is Phil Seeton still in room two-seventeen?" Shandra asked.

"Yes. He was having a difficult day but this will cheer him up," the nurse said, smiling and shaking her head.

"I hope so. Come on, Sheba." Shandra led her friend down the hallway, stopping when a resident held out a hand to pet Sheba.

They finally arrived at Phil's room. Shandra knocked, and opened the door, letting Sheba enter first.

"You're awful furry for a horse," Phil said.

Shandra entered and was surprised to see Phil in bed and not sitting in his recliner. His long nose and narrow face was void of color. His hand, petting Sheba, shook.

"Hi Mr. Seeton." Shandra pulled a chair up to the bed beside Sheba. "Do you remember me?"

"Edward's daughter. I didn't think I'd see you again." He smiled, but it looked like it took a lot of effort.

"Yes. How are you doing?" she asked, putting a hand on Sheba's back to make her sit.

"They say my body's failing me. I knew it would sooner or later. Too much drinking weakened my organs." He rubbed a hand across his forehead. "You look good. What's the name of this miniature pony?"

Shandra laughed. "That's what Lil said you would say."

Phil's mouth curved up on one side. "She did. How is she doing? Always liked that girl. A bit shy, but not nasty like the other girls hanging on the cowboys."

"She's fine. It's funny you mention girls hanging on cowboys. I came here to ask you what you remember about Jessie Preston. She was a barrel racer."

Phil was quiet for a time. Shandra wondered if he'd fallen asleep or was having that much difficulty remembering back so far. But his hand on Sheba's head slowly moved back and forth.

"Jessie was a fine barrel racer. She could have made some money if she hadn't slept around so much.

She was one of those women that they call a stalker today. She'd set her sights on a cowboy, and if he gave her the time of day, he was stuck with her until he either throwed her out or found a way to make her not like him anymore."

"I heard she was partial to Native American cowboys. And she liked my father but he ignored her." Shandra watched Phil.

He nodded. "Yeah, she did like the Indians. I don't know about Edward other than, I know he didn't care for her. It was because she'd get so tangled up in the cowboy she was with he couldn't keep his head on when he rode. Your father was all about making the next ride better than the last."

"Was she vindictive?"

Phil stared at her. "You think she caused Edward's death?"

"She made a comment that has me puzzled."

"You've talked to her? What's she look like now?" Phil shoved his body up a little higher in the bed.

Shandra stood and shoved pillows behind him to help him sit up.

"I had a short conversation with her in the Ketch Pen Tavern on the Colville Reservation."

"She marry an Indian?" Phil asked.

"Raymond Lawyer."

"Never heard of him. What's she doing?"

"She's training barrel horses. Has some videos and teaches classes." Shandra had been surprised at the woman's business sense.

"She knew her horses. Good for her." He squinted at Shandra. "But you suspect her?"

"I don't know. When I brought up Father she got upset and flung a bottle across the bar. I don't know what to make of it. Then I saw a photo of her and Dicky Harmond. They looked close."

Phil shook his head. "No. I can't see Jessie being with Dicky. He knocked women around. Jessie wouldn't put up with that."

"What about my mother. Did Dicky ever lay a hand on her?" She could see her mother being bossed around. She allowed Adam to run her life, but as far as she knew he'd never laid a hand on Celeste.

"If I remember right, Edward did stop Dicky from hurting your mom. There'd been a lot of drinking going on after a long weekend rodeo. The boys were celebrating their wins. As usual Edward was sipping on a beer, sitting in a corner away from all the rowdiness. Dicky came in already drunk and had a couple more. Celeste had talked with your dad, then was wandering around the place like she was looking for someone. Dicky grabbed her and took her for a round on the dance floor. I remember because he was whooping and causing a scene so everyone would see he had the princess on the floor."

Shandra stared at Phil. Jessie called her mother the same thing. "Why did you call my mother the princess? Jessie said the same thing."

Phil's cheeks added some color, a tint of red. "Everyone called Celeste the princess because she dated the prince. Adam Malcolm. He was the upcoming heir in the M Ranch Rough Stock Company. They both acted like they were better than everyone else associated with rodeo so we called them the prince and princess."

Shandra was getting a better glimpse into her mother. And it was clearing up a lot about how she'd perceived her mother while growing up. She thought back to what Phil had said. "Could Mother have been looking for Adam? You say she was walking around like she was looking for someone."

"It could have been him. It was rare for her to enter a bar without him by her side." Phil patted Sheba's head. "It was a while later when someone shouted 'Fight in the parking lot'. We all ran out and found Edward beating the tar out of Dicky and the princess leaning against a car her shirt torn." He shook his head. "It didn't take much sobering to figure out what had happened. Dicky took Celeste out into the parking lot to take advantage of her and Edward either came along or followed to keep her safe." He pointed a finger at Shandra. "It was after that night that we started seeing Celeste and Edward together. Your father was the princess's white knight."

Chapter Fourteen

Shandra drove home on auto-pilot as Phil's story played over and over in her head. Her father saved her mother from a nasty cowboy and she fell for his chivalrous nature. But where had Adam been? And did her mother take back up with him before or after her father's death?

"Maybe I should spend the night after the rodeo party so I can confront the two of them with the information I have." It was becoming clear that her mother and Adam had been keeping a lot of information from her. She wanted answers. Calling on the phone wouldn't get them. Her mother would redirect the conversation or hang up on her. No, it would have to be in person.

The information had also given her another person who would have had a grudge against Father. Dicky

Harmond.

She pulled up her driveway and her heart lifted seeing the Christmas lights Lil had put on the buildings. This was the first year they'd had lights. The other winters they'd been too busy trying to get things ready for winter and it would hit while they were still getting ready. This year they'd started earlier and had the time to do the extras, like string Christmas lights.

Ryan wanted to get a Christmas tree with her. She did traipse out in the woods last winter and cut down a small four-foot tree to put on the dining room table. With Ryan to help, they could get a tree befitting the vaulted ceiling in the living room.

She pulled up in front of the barn. Lil didn't open the doors. A bit surprised, but figuring she must be busy with a chore, Shandra stepped out and opened the barn doors. The interior was dark.

Flicking on the barn lights, she noted the horses weren't in the stalls for the night. Where could Lil be? It wasn't like her to not do the chores.

A low, distressed *mrowl* came from the direction of the tack room. Shandra opened the door and Lewis bolted out. Lil wasn't in the room. The lights weren't on.

Shandra hurried back to the Jeep and opened the back door. "Come on, Sheba. Go find Lil." Shandra let Sheba out, and she started running around in front of the barn, she disappeared into the trees and Shandra lost sight of her. It didn't make sense that Lil would be in the woods. Shandra pulled the Jeep into the barn and started to close the barn doors.

Howling caught her attention. Listening, she

distinguished it was Sheba. But it didn't come from the woods. The sound came from behind the barn. Shandra grabbed the flashlight in the emergency kit in the back of the Jeep and headed down the side of the barn. The howling became louder and her light caught the images of Sheba standing over someone, her muzzle pointed to the sky as she howled.

Shandra lunged through the several feet of snow to get to the back of the barn. On her back, in the snow, beside the corral fence, Lil was flat on her back. Her right leg was caught between the snow and one of the boards on the fence.

"I knew you'd show up," she said. Her pale color scared Shandra.

Lil needed to get in where it was warm. And she needed medical attention. She knew Lil would be angry but her best option was to call for an ambulance. She'd wait to dislodge the leg until she had a way to move her.

"I'm going to get a tarp to put you on, so I can pull you into the barn where it's warmer," Shandra told Lil. "Sheba, stay with her."

The large dog had already lain down next to Lil, using her fur and body to offer warmth.

Shandra followed the path she'd made the first time through the three-foot snow. In the barn she dialed 9-1-1.

"Nine-one-one what is your emergency?"

"This is Shandra Higheagle at four-four- two- one County Road Fifteen. I have a woman in her sixties who has a broken leg and has been lying in the snow for several hours."

"Keep her warm and we'll send an ambulance right out."

"Thank you." Shandra cut off the call and grabbed the first tarp she could find and two blankets out of Lil's room. The path to the back of the barn was getting easier to navigate the more times she trampled the snow down.

At the corner, she shone the light on Lil again, trying to figure out the best way to get her leg dislodged and her on the tarp without hurting her leg worse.

"Lil. I can pull you onto the tarp. I'm at a loss what to do to get your leg loose." Shandra directed the light to the leg.

Lil reached down, feeling her leg. "I think it will come free if you pull on me. I don't care about the leg right now."

"You might feel different later if I do something that makes it impossible for you to ride a horse again." Shandra didn't want to make the break worse.

"You won't make it worse. Just drag me onto that tarp. My back side is getting numb along with my fingers and toes."

Shandra grabbed Lil under her arms and dragged her onto the tarp. The leg did slide free of the fence.

Lil cried out when her leg straightened during the dragging.

Shandra's stomach churned with regret. But she continued dragging the smaller woman onto the tarp, and then tied one of the strings to Sheba's harness and grasped the other corner and the two of them pulled Lil over the uneven ground made from her previous tracks. She dragged Lil all the way into the barn.

Lewis meowed and laid across Lil's neck. She rubbed his back. "I know. You didn't get your nightly carousing of the barn."

"What happened?" Shandra asked, closing the doors.

"I went out to get the horses in for the night and spotted what looked like a stray cat behind the barn. I should have called to it instead of trying to catch it. I climbed over the corral fence and slipped. My right leg broke and I couldn't get up." Lil laid a forearm across her eyes. "I'm an old fool."

"You're not an old fool. You knew I'd be back. Sheba found you and we'll have you fixed up."

The sound of sirens grew.

Lil removed her arm and glared at Shandra. "Did you call an ambulance?"

"I did. It's the quickest, safest way to get you medical care." Shandra stood. "I'll direct them to the barn."

"You know how I feel about hospitals," Lil called as Shandra walked out the open barn door.

She ignored the woman. Lil had a phobia of hospitals, but Shandra wasn't going to shirk on the woman's care. Besides there wasn't a hospital in Huckleberry, only an emergency room.

To her surprise, Ryan's SUV pulled up to the barn. He stepped out and hurried to her.

"I heard the call. How's Lil?" He put an arm around Shandra, giving her support if she wanted it.

"Mad I called the ambulance. She'll live but I'm not sure how bad she broke her leg." Shandra slipped out of his embrace as the lights of the ambulance appeared in the meadow.

"Where is she?" Ryan pulled out his notepad.

"In the barn. Sheba found her behind the barn. She'd tried to climb the corral fence and her leg slid through." Shandra cringed at the thought of how the break must have occurred.

"Did you find her because she yelled?" Ryan watched her.

"No. I took Sheba with me to Missoula today."

"Missoula? Why'd you go there?"

The ambulance stopped and two paramedics ran up to them.

"She's in there," Shandra said, pointing inside the barn.

The paramedics ran on by.

"I was in Missoula visiting Phil Seeton. After what he told me, I'm thinking we may need to take my mother up on her offer of us spending the night after the party. I have some questions I'm pretty sure she won't want me to ask during the party."

"Miss Higheagle?" one of the paramedics called.

Shandra hurried into the barn followed by Ryan.

"Tell these two boys, I don't want to go to the hospital." Lil had a belligerent set to her face.

"Can you fix her leg here?" Shandra asked, already knowing the answer.

"No, ma'am," said the other paramedic.

"You have to go to the emergency room to get that leg set. I'll follow behind and bring you home as soon as Dr. Porter lets you." Shandra motioned to the paramedics. "Go ahead and take her in. I'll be right behind."

The two men picked up the stretcher. Shandra lifted Lewis from around Lil's neck.

"That's why I don't want to go to the Emergency. Lewis can't come with me," Lil complained.

"He'll be fine. You'll be home before morning." Shandra deposited Lewis back in the tack room as Lil was carried off telling the paramedics they didn't have the right to haul her around.

"I can drive you down to the Emergency," Ryan said.

"Then you'd have to bring me and Lil home afterwards. I better take my Jeep. But you can follow and buy me dinner. I'm hungry." Shandra opened the back door of the Jeep. "Come on, Sheba. You get to go for another ride."

The dog hopped in, happy to get two rides in one day.

"I'll close the barn doors behind you," Ryan said, as Shandra slid behind the steering wheel of the Jeep.

"Thanks. See you at the Emergency Room." She started the vehicle and backed out of the barn. Ryan closed the doors as she turned around. It was a comfort to see his lights in her rearview mirror as she drove down her lane and out to the county road. After the driving she did today, she hadn't wanted to drive herself, but it would have been selfish to have Ryan bring her and Lil back up the mountain tonight.

At the Emergency, she walked through the doors and found Dr. Porter and Maisie Granger already talking to Lil. Dr. Porter was close to Shandra's age and height, slender, with white hair and eyebrows and light blue eyes. His doctoring skills far surpassed what the community of Huckleberry needed, but he practiced here to be near his elderly great-aunt. Maisie was in her fifties and had the body of a stuffed bear and the cuddly personality to go with it.

"I'll pay for any expenses," Shandra said, walking up behind them.

"Shandra. Lil tells me she was climbing a fence when this happened," Dr. Porter said.

"That's what she told me. I wasn't there. But I came home in time to keep her from freezing to death." Shandra gripped one of Lil's hands. It was still cold but not as cold as when she'd first found the woman.

"We'll be at least a couple hours," Dr. Porter said, looking over her shoulder. "I think I know of a way you can pass the time." He nodded to the doors.

Shandra turned. Ryan strode toward them. "He's taking me to dinner," Shandra said. "Lil behave. I'll be back in two hours. If Dr. Porter says you can go home, I'll take you then."

"I guess I don't have much of a choice." Lil pouted.

"No, you don't. When Shandra comes back, I need your account of what happened," Ryan said before facing Shandra toward the door and moving her along with his hand on her lower back.

Chapter Fifteen

The air was cold but Ryan opted to walk to Ruthie's. It gave him more time to talk to Shandra without others around.

"What were you saying back at your place about spending the night with your parents?" Ryan had been spinning that around in his head all the way down the mountain. First she was taking him as a guest to her parents' party and now she said they would spend the night. He wanted to think Shandra's plan had to do with him getting to know her family better, but he doubted that was her reason.

"I need to ask them about Dicky Harmond attacking Mother and my father saving her. I have to know if gratitude for that was the only reason she slept with him and then stayed with him." Shandra sighed. "I can't ask them that with a room full of guests."

"So you want to spend the night? Or even attend the party?" Ryan asked. He'd received mixed messages from her acceptance to attend the dinner since she'd first mentioned it.

"No. I don't want to go. I only said yes to ask Mother and Adam questions." Shandra stopped a few doors down from Ruthies. "Adam only wants me there to make him look good to a new rodeo committee member." She scowled. "He only allows me to show my heritage if it's to his benefit."

"Then what if we go earlier in the day. Talk to them before the party. You're pretty sure they'll be upset. That means we won't have to stay for the party." Ryan knew it was underhanded, but he would rather see Shandra's mother and stepfather in their natural environment and not surrounded by people they were trying to impress.

Shandra hugged him. "That's perfect!" She grabbed his hand. "I'm starving."

They entered Ruthie's holding hands. Ryan liked that Shandra was slowly allowing their relationship to show to others.

Maxwell Treat, the son of the local mortuary owner who worked as a mortician and was on the Sherriff's Posse, waved them over to a booth where he sat. Treat and Ruthie were engaged, and the man spent every minute he wasn't working in the café.

"The detective and the artist. You two are looking cozy." Treat smiled big, his white teeth shining in his dark face and offered them the bench across from him. He took up half of his seat with his broad shoulders. He was over six foot and all muscle. An asset when the

Sheriff's Posse needed to haul someone out of the wilderness.

Usually Ryan would have avoided company when he had so little time with Shandra, but they would see each other Monday and Tuesday and the following weekend. He'd allow the man to cut in on some of his time.

"Thank you, Maxwell," Shandra said, sliding into the booth and scooting clear to the wall making room for Ryan.

"You on a date or working together?" Treat asked as Ruthie sauntered over, carrying glasses of water and the menus.

"Lil broke her leg," Shandra said. "We're waiting for Dr. Porter to get it set."

"How did she do that?" Ruthie asked, placing the menus and water in front of them and sliding into the booth alongside Treat.

Shandra retold how she found Lil.

"Poor thing. Will she be staying in the clinic overnight? I can take her some breakfast in the morning," Ruthie volunteered.

"No. I'm sure she'll be going home with me." Shandra picked up the menu. "After the day I've had, I think having my usual would be comforting. Cheeseburger, sweet potato fries, and a caramel shake, please." Shandra set the menu on the end of the table.

"And for you, Ryan?" Ruthie asked.

"I'll have cheeseburger, regular fries, and coffee. I'm still on duty and need to stay awake." Ryan set his menu on Shandra's.

Ruthie picked them up as she stood. "I'll have that

right out for you."

Treat watched Ruthie as she walked away.

"When are you two going to get married?" Shandra asked, taking the words out of Ryan's mouth.

Treat smiled. "Soon as I can persuade her living above the restaurant may be convenient, but it also puts you at work twenty-four-seven. I want her to have down time." He leaned in. "There's a place out your way, on county fifteen that is going on the market. I told Sam over at the realty office to not show it to anyone else until I get Ruthie to look at it." His whole face glowed. "She will love it!"

"Love what?" Ruthie asked, placing Ryan's coffee and Shandra's shake on the table.

"It's a surprise," Shandra said, her eyes shining.

Ryan liked how the serious Shandra could become dreamy-eyed, and all for a friend.

Ruthie studied Treat. He raised his eyebrows a couple of times and continued smiling like a man who had everything.

"He can't keep a secret. I'll find out soon enough what he's up to." She pivoted and headed back to the kitchen.

Treat's smile faded. "She's right. I can't keep nothin' from her."

Shandra laughed. "I'm sure this time you can because it means your futures." She enjoyed watching the interactions between Maxwell and Ruthie. They were two people in love and not afraid to let anyone see. She'd not had that kind of relationship with a man. What would it feel like for everyone to know you loved someone and they loved you?

Maxwell slid out of the booth. "Going to see if I can help Ruthie."

"Why do you look so serious? Are you worried about Lil?" Ryan asked.

"Yes. I wonder how much help she's going to need." She'd forgotten about Lil but didn't want Ryan to know she was contemplating her relationship.

"Knowing that woman, she'll insist on staying in her room in the barn and doing her chores." Ryan smiled and sipped his coffee.

"True. That's what worries me. I think I'll keep her in the house with me until you arrive on Monday. That way she can't sneak off and do the chores."

Ryan laughed. "That's a good idea."

Maxwell arrived with their plates of food. "You two are having a good time." He placed the plates in front of them.

"Talking about how Shandra's going to keep Lil chained to a bed while her leg heals," Ryan said.

"That I'd like to see." Maxwell laughed.

"Laugh all you want. You're not the ones who will have to deal with her." Shandra picked up a fry and nibbled on it. Not only did she need to do some digging on the computer, she'd have to contend with Lil's less than sunny disposition.

Maxwell wandered back to the kitchen. Shandra picked up her burger and asked Ryan, "Have you had a chance to check out Dicky Harmond?"

"No. This weather has had me out of the station all day. I was hoping to get on the computer at the end of shift." He swirled a fry in ketchup. "You said something about him attacking your mom?"

"Yeah, I guess he had a thing about knocking around women to get what he wanted. He picked the wrong woman one night. I'm still unclear as to why she was in a bar alone and why my father followed her and Dicky out to the parking lot. But according to Phil, that's what happened and when the crowd heard there was a fight, they all went out and found my father beating up Dicky and my mother's clothing ripped."

Shandra peered into Ryan's eyes. "Dicky could have tried to get revenge by killing father and making mother a widow. But everyone knew she'd been dating Adam. Unless Adam's prejudice toward Native Americans was so vocal, Dicky didn't think Adam would take Mother back…" she liked this line of thinking. It did meld well with what she knew of Adam. He was adamant he was right and it would take a lot of talking and persuading to get him to change his mind on a subject. Did her mother have that much pull with him to change his mind about her?

"If this Harmond is as violent as he sounds, I'm sure I'll come up with a record on him somewhere." Ryan took a sip of coffee before turning his head and studying her. "Have you found any proof that your father's accident was anything else? It's one thing to be drudging up all this information about who had grudges but in the end, if it was an accident…it all doesn't mean much."

This was where Shandra had to be persuasive. "How do I go about getting a file opened up to have the forensics rerun?"

Ryan didn't say anything for several minutes. "I don't think there's a thing you can do to get the autopsy records looked at unless you have proof there was a murder committed."

His words felt like a challenge. "I have to prove there was a murder before they will even open the case back up? That means I have to get someone to confess."

Ryan nodded. "Unfortunately the records won't be opened without a good reason to do so."

They finished the burgers and walked back to the clinic and emergency care facility. Walking through the door, Lil's voice carried down the hall.

"Call Shandra and tell her I'm ready to go."

"Lil. I'm not done. As soon as we have your leg properly cast and given you pain killers, you may go." Dr. Porter sounded like he was getting tired of being nice.

Lil had a way of wearing on people. And not in a good way.

"I'll see you Monday," Shandra said to Ryan. "I better go keep things civil between Lil and Dr. Porter."

"It sounds like Porter needs some help." Ryan leaned, kissing her cheek. "See you Monday. I'll get Lil's statement then."

Watching Ryan walk out the door, she wished he were coming home with her and helping with the obstinate woman, now calling Dr. Porter names. Shandra rushed down the hall, finding the room with no trouble.

"Lil, behave yourself. Dr. Porter is only trying to help." Shandra stepped up to the bed and took Lil's hand. She felt tremors in the small fingers and realized Lil's nastiness came from fear.

While Dr. Porter finished up, Lil was quiet.

Shandra stayed by her side and started wondering if Lil had ever been to a doctor before. Her miscarriage had happened on the mountain and no one had known about it. The way the woman remained a recluse most of her life, Shandra had a pretty good idea, Lil was more naïve than she'd first thought.

Forty-five minutes later, Dr. Porter wheeled Lil out to Shandra's Jeep in a wheel chair. Sheba stuck her head between the seats when the door was opened.

"Is that a bear?" Dr. Porter asked.

"That's a dog. If you can't tell that, you shouldn't be fixing people up," Lil retorted.

"She's Newfoundland and Border Collie. Or, so she was advertised. I have a feeling there is another large breed mixed in," Shandra said. She helped ease Lil into the passenger seat. Sheba licked the side of Lil's face.

"I think she's happy you're up and around," Shandra said.

"I don't need a bath," Lil said but with more warmth than anything she'd said to poor Dr. Porter.

"Like I said, it's a clean break. Keep the leg elevated for forty-eight hours. After that she can use these crutches to get around, but I'd advise to stay inside. With the snow and weather, she's more likely to slip and break something else if she's hobbling around outside. If the leg swells, elevate." He handed Shandra a small envelope of pills. "If she gets too ornery and you think it's from pain, crush one of these and put it in a drink."

Shandra stared at Dr. Porter. "You mean drug her without her knowing? You can do that?"

"If the pill is a powder and in something with enough flavor to mask it, yes."

Shandra shut the Jeep door and glanced around, relieved to see the nurse had returned to the warm building. "Dr. Porter, as a coroner in Weippe County could you request coroner records from other counties and states?"

"If I've heard of a similar death, I can. Why?" He watched her closely.

"I don't think my father's death was an accident. I've had a couple people explain what happened that day, and it sounds to me like he was drugged before he got on that horse." She shoved the pills in her pocket. "I was wondering if you could get the records and see if he had any drugs in his system?"

"Your record on helping solve murders is pretty convincing to me that you may be on to something. I'll see what I can dig up."

"Thank you. Don't tell anyone this is what I believe. It's all just me digging into the past. And thank you for putting up with Lil. She only acts that belligerent when she's scared."

"I figured, but it does get trying after an hour or so. Good night." Dr. Porter hurried through the emergency room doors.

Shandra climbed into the Jeep and headed toward home. With Dr. Porter checking on the coroner's report for her and Ryan digging up information on Dicky Harmond, she would start putting everything she knew into columns and see who wanted her father dead more than anyone else.

Murderous Secrets

Chapter Sixteen

Over the weekend Shandra had a reoccurring dream. Ella sat in the middle of an open area. Three triangles spun about her, dropping on points and bouncing. Faces flashed in and out of the points. Faces she was beginning to know. Dicky, her father, her mother, Adam, Charlie, Jessie, and a woman she didn't know. The faces faded and emerged as the triangles bounced and rolled.

She didn't know what it meant but knew with Ella in the middle of the chaos, it meant something.

Monday morning, Shandra helped Lil hobble from the guest room in the house out to Lil's room in the barn. She'd been complaining that at least in the barn she could find things to do. In the house there wasn't anything she could do that didn't involve walking. Lil wasn't happy if she wasn't busy.

With Lil settled in the barn, happily cleaning tack, Shandra pulled the sheets on the guest bed and tossed them in the washing machine. She wasn't sure when Ryan would arrive, he'd been busy the last few days and they'd barely talked. As of last night, he was still waiting on information about Dicky Harmond from law enforcement in two states.

She had tuna salad for lunch and had pulled steaks from the freezer the night before. Ryan liked steak and she grew up with beef for every dinner. Adam had refused to see anything else on his table. She narrowed her eyes. It's no wonder I allowed Carl to manipulate me and run my life, that's what my stepfather did from the moment he married Mother. He did it to me and to Mother.

Could he have orchestrated the fall that killed Father?

Sitting on the couch, she pulled her laptop onto her lap and continued her digging into the people associated with the rodeo where her father lost his life. She'd found out who the secretary was during that time and now needed to find out how to contact her. There had to be a way that her father ended up riding a horse known to stomp the rider if he hit the ground.

She'd entered the name in every conceivable search engine she could think of. The woman led an isolated life or she was no longer alive. The later bothered Shandra. If the woman was alive there was always a way to find her and talk to her, but if she was dead…

Shandra paid the fee for the online search of the woman and stepped into the kitchen to replenish her tea while she waited to see if the search revealed anything.

Sheba barked and the sound of wheels crunching in the snow made Shandra smile. Ryan had arrived.

She wandered to the front door.

"Hey, Sheba, what are you doing out in this?" Ryan asked. He stomped his boots and Shandra opened the door.

"Hello." She stood back as he moved through the door with a small duffel bag over his shoulder.

"Where do you want me to put my boots?" he asked, standing in the entry.

"On the rug beside the hall tree." Shandra looked down at the snowballs clinging to the hair on Sheba. "Sheba, shower."

Sheba slunk down the hall and into the laundry room. Shandra followed. She had the shower installed in the room for the big dog. A large bathing stool stood in the middle of the shower.

"Up," Shandra ordered.

Sheba climbed up on the stool. Shandra used a wide-toothed comb to break up the balls of snow and comb out the rest. She didn't like to deny Sheba the fun of playing outside, but this was a chore she didn't like to do more than twice a day.

"She tolerates that well," Ryan said from the laundry room door.

"I've been doing this to her since she was a puppy. If she gets too dirty I give her a shower." Shandra ruffled the fluffy ears. "She knows the routine. Okay, girl, you can go."

"Woof!" Sheba jumped off the stool, slamming it against the shower wall and charged out of the room, shoving Ryan out of the doorway.

"She really likes getting that over with," he said.

Shandra laughed. "She knows she gets a treat for being still."

Ryan laughed too.

They wandered into the kitchen. Sheba sat with her nose pointed to the cupboard that held her treats.

"Let me guess, the third cupboard from the door has her treats in it," Ryan said.

"Yes. And she knows it." Shandra opened the cupboard and picked a treat. Sheba swallowed it without chewing. "If you weren't such a good girl about staying clean, you wouldn't be in the house."

Sheba woofed and headed into the great room.

"Tea, coffee, or hot chocolate?" Shandra asked, pouring hot water into a cup with her favorite blend of green and white tea.

"Coffee if you have some made." Ryan sat at the counter.

She filled a cup and slid it over to him. He had something on his mind. His brow was furrowed and his lips pensive.

"What did you discover about Dicky Harmond?" she asked, sitting on a chair beside him.

"He was one bad apple." Ryan faced her. "He's dead. There isn't any way to talk with him."

The news wasn't the worse she could have heard but it made that link harder to follow. "How?"

"His temper seemed to be his downfall. He was arrested multiple times for beating up women, two were his wives. And he was jailed for several barroom brawls. The last one, he didn't walk away from. That was ten years ago."

Shandra shook her head. "Given what we know about him, and we're strangers, why would two women marry him?"

"I don't know. The first one, Denise Collins, pressed charges when he beat her up so bad she lost the child she was carrying. And the second wife, Melody Dean, pressed charges against him when she ended up in the hospital, needing reconstructive surgery on her face."

Shandra shivered. How could a man be that mean. "I don't like him. I'm glad he's no longer alive to hurt more women." Then one of the names started repeating in her head. Melody Dean.

"That's the name of the secretary. Melody Dean." Shandra hurried into the great room, sat on the couch, and pulled her laptop onto her lap. "I'd started a search for her before you came."

Ryan sat on the couch beside her.

"It's done. Melody Dean married Dicky Harmond the same year my father died. In fact, a month later." She peered into Ryan's eyes. "Do you think that's a coincidence?"

"Who is Melody Dean that you are looking her up?"

"She was the secretary of the Western Stampede Rodeo Association. The rodeo where Father died. Phil said the only people in the room when the cowboys and horses are drawn and put together for the rides are the president of the association, the secretary, and the rough stock contractor."

Ryan took a sip of his coffee and stared at her over

the cup. "Was your stepfather the rough stock contractor?"

"His family provided the stock, but I'm not sure if he or his father was present for the drawing. That's part of why I wanted to contact the secretary. The president has been gone for over twelve years." Shandra read the information on the computer. "She's alive. Still lives in Fairview. Doesn't say if she works anywhere." Shandra scrolled down the information. "Here's a phone number." She stared at the number. "I can't see her in person right now. I have to be close by for Lil. But…I could call and see if she remembers that day."

She placed the laptop back on the table and shifted on the couch to face Ryan. "I'm not breaking any laws by asking her some questions about that day am I?"

Ryan tucked the dark brown loose strands of hair behind Shandra's ear. He liked that she confided in him. "Asking a woman about how horses and riders were chosen for a rodeo would not get you in trouble. But remember none of this is official. We can't use anything she says to help change the decision on your father's death being an accident."

"I know. But it might get me closer to discovering the truth."

Shandra reached for her phone. Jazz tunes jingled. She didn't know the number that was calling.

"Hello?"

"Shandra, this is Dr. Porter."

"Hi. I forgot you were going to call." Shandra picked up her tea and sipped.

"I know it took me longer to find the information than I thought. How's Lil doing today?"

"I moved her to her room today. She was getting antsy with nothing to do in my house."

"Make sure she doesn't hobble around too much. If the leg swells she needs to elevate it."

"I told her. But you know Lil." Shandra moved a note pad across the table and picked up a pen. "What did you find out?"

"There were elevated levels of benzodiazepine in his system. The coroner at the time asked and was told he'd had an injury and was using a muscle relaxer. Does this help?" Dr. Porter asked.

"Yes and no. Thank you." Shandra circled the name of the drug. Her mother would know if her father was taking anything for an injury. But would Aunt Jo also know?

"What was that all about?" Ryan asked, turning the note pad toward him. "Benzodiazepine? Isn't that a narcotic?"

"Yes. It was in Father's system when they did the autopsy." Shandra scrolled through her contacts.

"How did Dr. Porter get information from your father's thirty-year-old coroner's report?" Ryan settled back against the couch cushions.

"I asked if he could access reports from other states and he said he could try. I guess he could." Shandra touched the name she wanted to call.

Several rings tolled in her ear before Aunt Jo answered out of breath. "Hello?"

"Hi Aunt Jo. It's Shandra. I have a couple questions about Father."

"Did you learn some more about his accident?" Aunt Jo asked.

"Yes. Was Father hurt before his accident? Enough to need pain killers?" Shandra studied Ryan's face, waiting for her aunt to answer.

"Not that I know of. As far as I know the only times he fell off a horse he didn't get more than bruised. Why?"

Shandra didn't want to get things stirred up. "I'll explain later. Thanks." She hung up before Aunt Jo could ask any more questions.

"Someone lied to the coroner. According to Aunt Jo, Father never had an injury bad enough to need medicine." She glanced down at the computer. Melody Dean's name and phone number popped out at her.

"Are you planning to call Dicky's second wife?" Ryan stood. He had his coffee cup and picked up her nearly empty tea cup.

"Yes. I need more information."

"I'll fill these and be right back." Ryan sauntered out of the room.

Shandra knew she should wait for him to come back before calling but she was on a roll and had to find out who was lying and why.

She dialed the number and waited.

"Hello?" A voice younger than she'd imagined answered the phone.

"Hello, I'm Shandra Higheagle. I'm trying to get in contact with Melody Dean. Or it might be Melody Harmond."

"My great-aunt doesn't live here. We put her in a nursing home three months ago."

"I see. Could you tell me what nursing home or give me a number I can reach her?" Shandra wasn't backing down now. She had to know the truth.

"Why do you need to talk to my great-aunt? She doesn't like visitors."

"I have some questions for her about a rodeo she helped with many years ago." Shandra didn't want to tell the whole story. The information she'd gathered so far could unravel at any time.

"She may not remember. Her memory is slowly getting worse."

"I'll take that chance. Do you have a phone number?" Shandra grabbed up her pen as Ryan returned with their refilled cups.

"She's at the West Ridge retirement home in Sunnyside, Washington. It's close to my mom."

"Thank you! This means a lot to me." Shandra hung up the phone and pulled up an app to see how long it would take her to get to Sunnyside, Washington.

"Ugh! Five hours."

"I have today and tomorrow free. I can drive." Ryan put a hand on her leg.

"But I can't leave Lil alone for that long." This was one time when she wished she didn't live so far from other people.

"Does she have a friend you could have stay with her overnight?" Ryan picked up his cup of coffee.

"No. The only person I can think of is Maxwell."

Ryan spit coffee on his shirt. "Treat? Why would he want to spend the night here with Lil?"

"He may not, but he's the only person I know big enough and strong enough to make her do things." Shandra smiled. It would be fun to watch the two of them butting heads.

"She doesn't have anyone her age who could come play cards with her and keep her company?" Ryan had a look of disbelief.

"She's never made friends. Her only true friend was Sally Albright, but she's living with her niece." Shandra shook her head. "I can't think of anyone else."

Ryan sat up. "I'll see if Hazel Wells would come out."

Chapter Seventeen

Ryan sat in his pickup waiting for Shandra to give Hazel the last instructions about Lil. They'd moved Crazy Lil back into the guest room so Hazel wouldn't have to sit in the barn with the curmudgeon. He'd been in luck. Hazel had taken several days off from dispatching at the Huckleberry Police Station to take care of Christmas projects and was willing to sit with Lil.

Shandra carried an overnight bag as she approached the vehicle. She smiled as she climbed in the passenger seat. "Those two are already playing cards. I'm glad you thought of Hazel."

"Me, too. We should get to Sunnyside by dark. We can get settled for the night then talk with Melody first thing in the morning." Ryan turned his pickup around and headed down the driveway.

135

Shandra placed a hand on his arm. "I hope you don't mind doing this on your days off."

He put a hand over hers. "As long as I'm spending my days off with you, I don't care what we do." Lifting her hand, he kissed the back.

She smiled and slowly pulled her hand back. There was still a couple of layers he didn't know about the woman. He hoped discovering the truth about her father's death and her parents' relationship would help his future with her.

The storm that had made the roads so treacherous the last week had moved on. Snow piled alongside the main road out of Huckleberry, but Interstate 90 was clear. The conversation had lulls where they listened to the radio and then would pick up again on a new topic.

"How are your family?" Shandra asked.

"Fine. Mom, Bridget, and Cathleen keep asking me when I'm bringing you over for Sunday dinner." He figured that was better than asking her if she wanted to visit Christmas Day which was their real question.

"You go to your parents' house for Sunday dinner? Every week?" The surprise in her voice made him laugh.

"Not if I can help it. But they ask me every week if I'm coming." He shook his head. Still trying to figure out his mother and sisters. "In fact, they've been unrelenting since Conor and Lissa married. And use that they, Conor and Lissa, come to Sunday dinner every other Sunday." Even if he could sit through a meal every Sunday with his father badgering him about his career choice, he didn't think he could take watching the newlyweds be happy while he still wasn't ready to commit. He glanced over at Shandra. She watched him intently. When he was ready. He wanted her to be the bride.

"You said you were okay with Conor marrying your ex-girlfriend." She'd said the 'ex' part with emphasis.

"I am. I'm happy for both of them. I just don't want to sit through a meal watching them be so damn happy when I'm—" He stopped before he said damn lonely.

Shandra shoved her bag on the floor at her feet, unbuckled her seatbelt, and moved over, sitting beside him and buckling the center belt around her. "When you're what?"

He had to keep his eyes on the road even though he wanted to look into her eyes and see her reaction.

"So damn lonely." He said it and glanced over at Shandra.

Her face was tipped down. Then she looked over at him. He had to glance back at the road.

"I'm lonely, too. I'm happy. I love my life. But sometimes…Lil just isn't the one I want to recount my day to." She put a hand on his thigh. "You haven't used my invitation to stay at the ranch when you have a case in Huckleberry."

She didn't know how hard he'd wished for an assignment that would keep him in that area. "Nothing has come up since you extended the invitation." He put a hand over hers.

"You were going to help me get a Christmas tree. I guess it will have to wait."

"I'll be back on the weekend. We can get the tree

on Sunday. I won't have to head back to Warner until late in the day." He wanted to spend as much time with her as he could. Shandra helped chase away the loneliness.

"That could work." She sighed. "I honestly expect to be thrown out of Adam's house right after I ask my questions. I don't have any guarantee we'll get any answers." She turned her hand under his, lacing their fingers. "They've hidden the truth from me for this long, they aren't going to like me dredging up their past."

"Our families are complete opposites," Ryan said. "Mine tell each other way too much and yours don't say a thing."

Shandra nodded. "Did your family try to keep you from going into the military?"

"No. Dad was a little upset that I didn't want the sheep ranch, but when Cathleen's husband was interested, he was happy. Conor was never interested in the sheep either."

"First my mother and Adam wouldn't let me talk about or learn about my father's family, then they tried to keep me out of art classes. But I loved drawing and making things with my hands. It was my grandmother, the one who left me the money that allowed me to purchase the property on Huckleberry Mountain, who told me to follow what my heart said." She smiled. "She had her differences with my mother. But she was the one person who let me, as a child and adult, be me."

She leaned into him a bit. "That's what has drawn me to you. You allow me to be who I am."

"Everyone is different and it's that difference that

138

makes them unique." Ryan squeezed her hand. The sun had drifted out of sight over an hour earlier. The LED light on the dash said it was 5:30.

"We should be pulling into Sunnyside soon. You want to eat first or find a motel?"

Shandra put a hand on her belly. "Food. I haven't had anything since breakfast."

"You should have said something. We could have stopped along the way."

"I just wanted to get here. Once we're here there's nothing that can stop us from talking to Melody." That was Shandra's biggest fear. Not being able to talk to the one person she was sure had the answers.

"There's a chain restaurant. Want to try it?" Ryan pointed to the right.

"Yes."

While at the restaurant, they received directions to the nursing home and a clean motel.

Ryan stopped the pickup at the motel and turned to her. "This type of motel isn't the safest. I'd feel better if we had one room with two beds. Is that okay with you?"

Shandra had thought about this most of the way. She didn't like the idea of being in a strange town in a motel room by herself. Especially one with the doors open to the public. When she taught at colleges and attended art shows, she always booked the fancy hotels where there were doormen and cameras to catch unwanted people. "One room, two beds is fine."

"Ok. And I prefer upper floor, less likely to have some random hoodlum come by." Ryan eased out of the truck and looked up at the two-story structure.

"I agree. Upper."

"Got it. I'll be back in a few minutes." He closed the door.

Shandra shivered from the cold air that settled in the cab while he'd stood with the door open. Ryan didn't know it, but this was a test. He'd proven while staying at her place he could remain in his room and not try and sneak into her bed. Being in the same room all night would be a test for them both. She had a connection with Ryan. But she wanted to make sure he wouldn't try to control their relationship before she took it to the intimate stage.

Ryan returned. "Room two-eleven." He shut off the engine and grabbed his bag out of the toolbox in the back.

Shandra picked up her backpack and followed him up the stairs by the office and halfway down the covered walkway.

Ryan opened the door and flicked on the light. "Check it out. If it's not clean enough or you see anything you don't like, we'll look for another one."

He set his duffel bag on the bed closest to the door.

She lifted the covers, checking for hairs and dirt. They looked clean. She walked into the bathroom. It also appeared clean. "This will work," she said, dropping her backpack on the bed next to the bathroom wall.

Ryan clicked on the TV. "You want to shower or change or something?"

She glanced at the clock on the table between the beds. It was after nine. "I'll shower if you don't mind."

He smiled and reclined on his bed. "Take as long as

you want, looks like the Hawks are playing."

Shandra glanced at the TV. Football. She liked watching sports but didn't know much about anything but rodeo. Picking up her backpack, she wandered into the bathroom and closed and locked the door.

With Ryan watching TV on the bed next to the door, there was little chance of having an unexpected guest.

The bathroom was full of steam by the time she exited the bathroom. "It's all yours," she said, dropping her backpack on the floor by the TV and walking to her bed.

"I shower in the morning," Ryan said, turning off the TV. He'd changed into pajama bottoms and a T-shirt while she'd been showering. The shirt was tight.

She dropped her gaze to the light. "Good night."

Ryan turned the overhead lights off and laid down on the bed. He rolled her direction, his hand on the light switch. "Good night." The light went off and they were in the dark.

There was enough light shining through the curtains, his body was silhouetted. Shandra rolled with her back to Ryan. The dark wall was better.

He rolled.

She remained still listening for his breathing to even. Once she was sure Ryan had fallen asleep, she let her body relax and slowly drifted into the darkness of slumber.

An owl sat on a branch. It hooted at Shandra. She smiled and waved to the owl. But it turned into a hawk and soared out of the tree towards her. Shandra ran through the trees, trying to evade the hawk. It screeched and grabbed at her. She dropped to the ground, trying to hide next to a tree. The hawk landed in a branch and turned back into the owl.

Shandra waited and waited. Ella appeared and motioned for her to continue on her journey. Shandra cast a look at the owl. It remained on the limb. Quickly, hoping to get out of the bird's sight, Shandra ran through the trees. She came to a cliff. One thin pole lay across a deep canyon. Ella stood on the other side, motioning for her to come. Fear took over her body, making her shake and weep.

Wolves charged out of the trees. Shandra screamed and jumped off the cliff.

"Shandra, wake up. Shandra, honey, you're safe. I'm here."

Ryan's voice slowly lifted her up. Her hands grabbed the pole.

"Shandra, wake up. You're shaking. It's just a dream. Wake up."

Her shoulder shook, releasing her mind from the dream, and she floated awake. Her eyelids slowly fluttered open. The dim light from the bedside table illuminated one side of Ryan's face. Worry etched furrows in his brow and crinkled the lines around his eyes.

"That's it. Wake up." His hand pushed hair off her face and lingered on her cheek. "Was it a bad dream or a dream with your grandmother?" he asked in a low, husky voice.

"Both." She swallowed and shoved her body up to a sitting position.

Ryan straightened but remained sitting on the side

of the bed. "What do you mean by both?"

She told him about the owl turning into a hawk and Ella helping her get away, and then her fear to cross the small pole that Ella wanted her to cross and the wolves coming after her.

"I screamed when I jumped into the canyon." Her mind whirred to the image of her body lifting when she heard Ryan's voice. He had saved her. His concern had brought her out of the canyon just as it had awakened her, getting her away from the fear in her dream. She didn't tell him that part of the dream. She'd keep it to herself and see what she could make of it.

"Are most of your dreams with your grandmother scary?" He picked up her hand, holding it gently.

"No. This is the first one that made me feel threatened. The others she usually shows me where to find something or points a finger at someone." Shandra sat up straight. "Do you think she's telling me that I'm bringing danger to myself with my questions?" It scared her but it also meant her father was murdered if someone was worried about her questions.

Chapter Eighteen

The next morning, Shandra ate her breakfast with gusto as she and Ryan sat a small café between the motel and the nursing home. She knew Melody would help her discover the truth. This was the day she'd piece together the details of the day her father died.

Shandra glanced over at Ryan as they drove the last few blocks to the nursing home. "Do you feel Melody will have the answers?" she asked Ryan, hoping he'd be as optimistic.

"I think you wouldn't be digging this hard for the truth if your father's death had been an accident. As for what we find out today…" He shrugged. "We won't know until we talk to Mrs. Harmond."

They pulled into the nursing home at nine.

"I hope they've finished with their morning meal. I'd hate to interrupt her routine too much." Shandra shouldered her leather-fringed bag and walked beside Ryan into the one-story facility.

"May I help you?" a woman sitting at a reception desk asked.

"We'd like to visit with Melody Dean Harmond," Shandra said, not sure what name the woman went by.

"She's in one-twenty. Down the hall, make a right, and then a left, and you'll find her in the Alzheimer's wing." The woman smiled.

Ryan grasped Shandra's elbow and led her down the hall.

She stopped. "Alzheimers. She may not even remember being a secretary for the rodeo association." Disappointment lodged in her throat. All this work and they may not learn a thing.

"We won't know that until we talk with the woman." Ryan tugged on her arm. "You can't give up that easy."

Ryan was right. She wasn't giving up. They made the turns and stopped at a locked door. A small sign said to type in the year. Ryan did and the doors opened.

Inside the doors, sat another woman in a nurse's uniform. "May I help you?" she asked.

"We're here to see Melody Dean Harmond in room one-twenty," Shandra said.

The woman smiled. "You're in luck. She's having a good day and should remember you."

Shandra smiled at Ryan.

They continued down the hall and found the room. Shandra knocked on the door of one-twenty. A name plaque to the side said Melody Dean.

"Looks like she doesn't go by Harmond," Ryan

said as a voice called out, "Come in."

Shandra nodded and entered the room. The sight made her smile. There were rodeo posters and photos papering one wall of the small room. Melody sat in a wooden rocking chair beside a hospital bed with a western print quilt. The woman appeared to be able-bodied. She glanced up from her knitting as they walked into the room.

"Hello? Do I know you?" she asked, adjusting her glasses.

"No, Ms. Dean, you don't know us." Shandra snatched the wood chair sitting at a small table with puzzle pieces and sat in front of the rocking chair. "I'm Shandra Higheagle and this is my friend, Ryan Greer."

Ryan had pulled a foot stool up beside Shandra and sat.

"Higheagle?" The woman stared at her. "I remember a Higheagle on the rodeo circuit."

Shandra couldn't hide the grin ticking at her lips. "That was my father. Edward Higheagle. He rode bareback broncs."

"Yes. I remember. He was good. Rarely landed in the dirt." Melody smiled, then frowned. "But he did land in the dirt and that old Loco stomped him…" She raised a tissue to her mouth and her eyes watered. "That was a terrible day. Terrible."

"Try to forget about the ride. Do you remember earlier that day, when the horses and riders were drawn?" Shandra asked.

Melody lowered the tissue and stared at Shandra. "The drawing? It went as usual. Myself, the president at the time, Harold Lymen, and Mr. Malcom. It was his

146

stock we used that day."

Shandra nodded. "Mr. Malcolm, do you mean the father, Walter, or the son, Adam?"

Melody had dropped her knitting into her lap. Now, she held the yarn between two fingers on her right hand, moving her hand up and down the yarn six inches. "There were two Mr. Malcolms." She became agitated. "Harold said it was fine. But we'd never had more than the three of us in the office drawing before. Harold pulled out the cowboy names and Mr. Malcolm the animal."

"I understand that's how it worked. Was there anything different that day besides the two Mr. Malcolms?" Shandra asked.

"Dicky hit me." Melody flinched as if she'd been struck.

"Why did he hit you?" Shandra asked, sorry to have brought up painful memories. But if it had to do with her father's death she needed to know.

"Because I said we should tell someone." Her fingers moved faster up and down the yarn.

"Tell them what?" Shandra persisted.

"That the drawing had been different." Melody didn't look at her.

"Different how?" Shandra leaned forward, urging the woman to remember.

"Both Mr. Malcolms drew the animals, and I saw a piece of paper fall on the floor. After the drawing, when the Malcolms and Harold left to post the rides, I picked it up. It was one of the bareback horses."

"Who are you?" a woman's voice demanded.

Shandra shot to her feet.

147

Ryan stood slower and extended his hand. "Ryan Greer and this is Shandra Higheagle." He'd let Shandra do the questioning. The woman had seemed more at ease with her. He could tell Shandra was still stunned and processing what she'd heard. He'd deal with the woman who had arrived.

He waited for the woman to put her hand in his. "And you are?"

"Marsha Smith, Melody's niece." She bypassed his extended hand and stood by her aunt.

"What do you want with my aunt?" she asked, putting a protective hand on the older woman's shoulder.

"We were asking her about her days as a rodeo secretary." Ryan put his hand on Shandra's lower back, leading her to the exit. "Good day, Ms. Dean," he said.

Shandra stopped. She walked away from him and back to the woman in the chair. "Thank you. I hope you have a wonderful day." She patted the woman's hand and returned to the door.

Ryan ushered her out and down the hall. He didn't start a conversation until they were inside his pickup.

"That is pretty damning information against your stepfather. She'd have to tell a prosecutor, and I don't think her memory will hold up in court." He didn't want to hit Shandra with the reality of what they'd discovered, but he had to before she thought they could run to officials.

"I understand. What I don't understand is why would Dicky hit her because she told him she suspected something was amiss? I'm pretty sure Adam had Loco's name up his sleeve to pretend to pick when father's name came up. But who drugged my father? There had to be more than one person involved for this to have gone off as easily as it did."

Ryan didn't want to say the obvious person who drugged her father was her mother. "I guess we have another question to ask your stepfather next Saturday." Ryan started the engine and backed out of the parking lot.

Shandra sat silently on the passenger side for nearly an hour. Ryan wasn't sure if he should intrude on her thoughts or let her be.

She finally turned toward him. "Dicky had to be the one who gave father the drugs. Why else would he want Melody to keep quiet? But what I don't get is why she didn't say anything all these years after leaving Dicky?"

"I don't know. Maybe after he beat her up, she repressed the information and then hearing the name triggered it." Ryan was grasping at reasons just as much as Shandra was. He was an officer of the law and as such felt he needed to follow up on this new information. Unfortunately, without proof and only Shandra's dreams to go on, his superior wasn't going to give him work hours to dig for information.

"That could be. It's as good a reason as any I guess." Shandra stared out the window for another twenty minutes.

"Do you think Dicky and Adam killed my father because of my mother?" Shandra's voice was barely above a whisper. As if she didn't want to state the vile thoughts she was having.

He reached across the cab, grasping Shandra's

hand. "There is a possibility your mother could be involved in your father's death." He squeezed her hand. "I'll be here for you whatever you need."

She studied his face. Tears sparkled in the corners of her eyes. "I've had a feeling for years that I hadn't been wanted. Then talking with Father's side of the family I learned Father and Ella wanted me, my mother would have snuffed out my life had she been allowed to do what she wanted."

Ryan saw a wide spot in the road and pulled over. This was a conversation that needed all his attention. Once the vehicle was in park, he pulled Shandra into his arms. "Your father and grandmother were right to fight for you. Your mother raised you when she could have sent you to the Higheagles. In her own way, I think she came to love you." Ryan smoothed Shandra's hair as she snuggled into his chest.

She sniffed and lifted her head. "I don't think she loves me. She has raised me to spite the Higheagles and her mother. And maybe even Adam." She shook her head. "I'm just a pawn."

Chapter Nineteen

Shandra remained in Ryan's arms, battling with the rage swirling inside. There was one more person who could have drugged father. The woman who had ran her life like a drill sergeant then introduced her to Professor Landers who tried to stomp out her self-worth and dignity.

"Thank you," Shandra said as she moved out of Ryan's arms. She had learned to stand on your own two feet and if it meant finding out her mother was an accomplice to her father's death, so be it.

"You okay?" Ryan asked, one hand still holding her arm.

"Yes. I realized there is another person who could have drugged my father." As she said the words and stared into Ryan's eyes, she saw that he'd come to the same conclusion.

"What do you plan to do about it?" he asked, studying her face.

"I plan to make a list of questions to ask both Mother and Adam on Saturday. I also plan to have it all recorded." Shandra settled back on her side of the seat.

Ryan put the pickup into drive and moved back onto the road.

Shandra was thankful Ryan drove and didn't ask questions. She had a lot to process in her mind. So many times over the years she'd tried to talk about Father or how he died and was always silenced. Either by her mother or Adam. Their actions were proof of guilty consciences.

About thirty minutes past Warner on Hwy 9 to Huckleberry, Ryan sat up straighter and started cussing.

"What—? Before Shandra could get the question out, a large truck jack-knifed in front of them on the highway.

"Hold on," Ryan swerved the pickup, missing the back end of the semi-truck's trailer by inches. The pickup shot off the road and slammed hard into the snow. The air bag deployed, slamming into Shandra's face and upper chest. As quickly as it inflated, the bag deflated.

Shandra wanted to take a deep breath but refrained with the white powder drifting in the air. Cold air stood the hair on her arms up. Ryan had shoved his door open.

"Are you all right?" he asked, stepping out of the vehicle.

"Yes. I don't feel like anything is broke." She moved her arms and unbuckled her seatbelt.

"I'm going to see what that truck driver thought he was doing. Call nine-one-one." Ryan disappeared back toward the highway.

The white dust was floating out the open door. She pulled on her coat and dialed 9-1-1.

"Nine-one-one, what is your emergency?" a female voice asked.

"A semi jack-knifed on Hwy 9 thirty minutes east of Warner. We were run off the road by the truck. An off duty Sheriff's deputy is checking on the driver."

"We'll send emergency vehicles. Please stay on the line."

Shandra put her phone on speaker and set it on the dash. The snow looked to be three feet deep outside the vehicle. "Do I dare try to get up to the highway or just stay put?" She wanted to check on Ryan but didn't want to cause him concern if she injured herself trying to climb up the small embankment they'd sailed down.

A tree not three feet in front of them started her heart racing all over again. They could have hit that tree and been injured much worse.

The phone crackled. "Help is ten minutes away."

"Thank you."

***

Ryan used his anger to forge his way up the embankment. That truck driver had been in their lane for no reason. He'd slammed on his brakes and skidded sideways leaving Ryan no choice but to bail off the interstate. That driver had damn well better have a good reason for his actions. Shandra could have been injured or killed. When the bag had deployed and he'd seen the large pine tree not three feet in front of the truck, his heart had stopped beating. Shandra moving and not showing any signs of injuries had squashed his concern and sent him after the cause of the crash.

He lunged onto the road, sucking air. The cold air stung his lungs, but he didn't care. The jack-knifed rig spouted smoke from the pipes. Cars had stopped on either side of the semi. Ryan strode toward the cab of the semi. The door stood open and the cab was empty. He climbed up the steps and shoved the curtain to the sleeping bunk back and an empty compartment. The bastard had run!

Ryan stepped down and headed to the first car in line. He motioned for the driver to roll his window down.

"Did you see where the driver went?" Ryan asked, pulling his badge out of his shirt pocket.

"Nope. The door was standing open when I came up to the truck." The man shivered. "Any idea how soon this will get cleared?"

Ryan glared at him. "No one will move until every car in this line has been questioned."

Sirens grew near. Ryan walked back to the edge of the road. His pickup was thirty yards down the embankment. It wasn't in harm of moving. The nose was planted firmly in the deep snow. But Shandra was down there.

He pulled out his phone and dialed her number.

"Did you get him?" she asked.

"No the truck was empty. Are you doing okay down there? I hear the emergency vehicles coming. Once I get them caught up on what happened I'll come down and get you." He saw the driver's side door close.

"I'll be fine. Do what you need to do." Her voice was strong.

She was strong.

A trait he admired in Shandra.

"I'll hurry."

Deputy Gerald Speaks walked around the end of the semi along with two paramedics.

"Greer, I thought today was your day off," Speaks said.

"It is. I was on my way back from Sunnyside with a friend and this semi was driving down my lane. When it jack-knifed, I swerved off the road, barely missing the back end." He nodded to the embankment. "We ended up about thirty yards down there." He glanced at the paramedics. He'd worked with both Paul Moore and Evelyn Cates before. "My passenger said she wasn't hurt, but if you could bring her up, I'd appreciate it."

They nodded and headed to the embankment.

"Where's the semi driver?" Speaks asked, walking toward the semi cab.

"Rabbited." Ryan spit the word out. "He must have a record or something to have left his rig running and the door standing open."

They walked to the side of the road at the front of the semi. Foot prints took off into the woods.

"I'll call in a State K-9 unit."

"I'm going to start questioning the people in the cars. You'll need to get a hold of someone to move the truck." Ryan left Speaks making calls on his radio and headed to the second car in line on the west side of the semi.

He'd questioned the occupants of the first five

vehicles when he spotted the paramedics and Shandra appear at the top of the embankment.

"I didn't know anyone was down there," the woman driving the sixth car in the line said.

"What did you see when you pulled up to the stopped cars?" Ryan asked.

"The semi across the road and the cars ahead of me. That's it." She looked perplexed. "Should I have seen more?"

"No." Ryan folded his book up and headed to Shandra. She was limping and using Evelyn to help her walk.

"I thought you said you didn't hurt yourself?" he questioned, stepping to Shandra's side and taking over from Evelyn.

"It must have been the shock or adrenaline from the crash. I didn't realize I'd sprained my ankle until we started up the embankment." She raised the fancy cowboy boot dangling in her hand. "They say I can't wear my boot until the swelling goes down."

Ryan caught Evelyn smiling with a look on her face his sisters and mother got every time Shandra's name came up.

"Can you sit her down in your rig until I get a tow truck and someone to pick us up?" Ryan asked Evelyn and Paul.

"We can take her to Warner," Paul said.

"No. I want to go home." Shandra peered up at Ryan. "Call Hazel. She can leave Lil long enough to come get me. You can get a ride back to Warner."

He didn't like sending her off with anyone when he wasn't sure how hurt she was physically, and mentally after the information they received today.

"I'll get another set of wheels and take you home." He walked her to the ambulance.

Evelyn opened the back for Shandra to sit.

"Keep her here until I get back," Ryan placed Shandra on the floor of the ambulance.

"If we get another call, we'll have to leave," Paul said.

"I understand. We'll move her to Speaks car if that happens." Ryan ran his hand down Shandra's arm. "We'll be on the way to your house soon."

She nodded and he left her to the paramedics.

He opened his contacts list and touched his mother's number.

"Hi Ryan. I was surprised you weren't home today. Wasn't it your day off?" His mother answered.

"It was my day off. I took a trip with Shandra—"

"Shandra! Oh, that's wonderful. How is she?" his mother cut-in.

"We had an accident. I was wondering if you and Dad could drive my Mustang to a roadblock about thirty miles east of Warner on Hwy 9."

"I thought you weren't going to drive that old car until you had the rag top fixed."

He ignored his mother's tone. "I don't have a choice. My truck is wrecked—"

"Are you okay? What about Shandra? Was she with you?" His mother once again interrupted him.

"We're fine. Shandra has a sprained ankle, but we're fine other than needing a vehicle to drive. Could you please come right away? It's cold and the ambulance needs to get back on call."

"Yes. We'll be there in half an hour."

His mom hung up. They wouldn't arrive any sooner than forty-five minutes given the road conditions and the fact the Mustang didn't have snow tires.

Chapter Twenty

Shandra watched Ryan. He had a phone conversation, then walked over and talked to the deputy she'd met when her neighbor was shot. She shivered. That was another event when Ella came to her in dreams, helping to solve that murder.

The cold seeped through the blanket, her clothes, her muscles, and deep into her bones. It was a cold that was both physical and mental. The woman paramedic had tried to make Shandra sit inside the ambulance with the doors closed. Shandra refused to go any farther in the vehicle than the back step. She wanted to see what was happening and not be carted away if she climbed into the vehicle any farther.

The radio in the ambulance crackled.

The male paramedic responded and called back to them, "We have a wreck on County Ten."

"We have to go. Keep the blanket, Ryan can get it back to us later." The woman paramedic helped Shandra onto her feet and closed the back doors of the ambulance.

The driver started up the lights.

Ryan glanced her way and walked toward her. "I guess they had to leave," he said, taking a hold of her arm and helping her walk over to the deputy's car. "I called my parents. They're bringing my other vehicle. Once they arrive I'll get you home."

He rubbed his hands up and down her arms.

Two State Patrolmen arrived.

Shandra leaned against Ryan to buffer the wind that had started up.

Ryan wrapped his arms around her.

The state patrolman in the front frowned. He stopped in front of them and nodded at Ryan's arms. "I wish I worked for the county and could hug pretty ladies while on the job."

Ryan chuckled. "I'm not on duty. We called this in since the truck blocking traffic is what ran us off the road."

A long line of cars waited on both sides of the truck.

The other patrolman flipped open his notebook. "Show me what happened."

"Can I put Shandra in one of your cars? She sprained her ankle in the crash and shouldn't walk around." Ryan slipped his arm under her knees, carrying her toward the patrol cars.

"I could walk," she said only loud enough for Ryan's ears.

"But you shouldn't. Stay here until our ride arrives. I'll get our things while I'm showing Pearce what happened."

The man Ryan called Pearce, opened the back door of his vehicle, and Ryan placed her inside. He tucked the ambulance blanket around her. "Should only be another twenty minutes and we'll get out of here."

He closed the door on her and walked away talking to the patrolman.

She scanned the area. A long line of cars waited on both sides of the truck. Where could the driver have gone? And why did he run? They may never know. But someone needed to arrive soon and move the truck. The traffic was piling up.

Cars started honking their horns in the direction of Warner. Shandra peered down the long line and saw two vehicles coming down the side of the road the patrolmen had used.

The patrolman that wasn't with Ryan strode forward. She could tell he wasn't pleased with whoever it was that had driven up to the scene.

The first vehicle was an SUV. The second looked like an older model Mustang with a blue tarp for the top.

Shandra's chin dropped when Mr. Greer stepped out of the Mustang and Mrs. Greer stepped out of the SUV. Shandra couldn't open the car from the inside. She sat wrapped in the warmth of the blanket and watched Ryan's parents.

Ryan's mom had an animated conversation with the patrolman. He pointed toward the car Shandra sat in. Mrs. Greer waved and headed her way. Mr. Greer conversed with the patrolman a moment then climbed back into the Mustang and drove it over to the patrol car.

Mrs. Greer opened the patrol car door. "Shandra, I'd hope to see you again but not under these circumstances. Come along. We'll get you in the Mustang." She grasped Shandra's arm, lifting her out of the patrol car.

"Ryan's over there—" Shandra started to say.

"I'm sure he's fine and doing what needs to be done," Mrs. Greer interrupted her. "Ephraim, get that passenger door open for Shandra."

Shandra was shuffled from one car to the other. She was skeptical of the tarp being used for the car's top, but the heater was on full blast and the inside of the Mustang was warm.

Mrs. Greer said something to her husband and slipped into the driver's side of the Mustang. "This is nice and warm. I don't know why Ryan didn't just have us pick you two up instead of insisting on us bringing him this old car."

"It's a classic. I didn't even know Ryan owned a Mustang," Shandra said, to keep the conversation on something other than their relationship.

"He bought this car in high school and has been slowly putting it back to its original state. He made sure the motor and transmission were fixed first. That way he can use it as a second vehicle when he needs to." Mrs. Greer twisted in the seat to face her. "Where did you two go today?"

Shandra knew the question was coming the moment she'd recognized Mrs. Greer climbing out of the SUV. "We took a trip to Washington." There was no need to tell Ryan's mom the reason behind the trip. Even though Mrs. Greer had taught Ryan to believe in things he couldn't see and gave him the ability to believe in Shandra's dreams.

"I see. Did you have a good time?" The woman's eyes sparkled with interest.

"I guess. I enjoy your son's company." Shandra peered into the woman's eyes. "Ryan and I are good friends who are getting closer."

Mrs. Greer's grin grew.

"But neither of us is ready to commit to each other or anyone. Please, stop pressuring Ryan."

The woman's eyes narrowed. "I see. Has Ryan said I'm pressuring him?"

Shandra shook her head. "No. But he's told me about conversations. He loves you and his whole family. But he needs space, not smothering."

Mrs. Greer looked over Shandra's shoulder. "Here he comes. I'll talk to you another time." Mrs. Greer slid out of the car.

Ryan walked up to his Mustang carrying his and Shandra's overnight bags. His mother stepped out of the driver's side. Shandra sat in the passenger seat. He groaned inwardly. What had his mom been telling Shandra?

"We brought your car," Mom said, walking toward him.

"Thank you." He walked around the back of the car and stopped in front of his mom. "I'll call you tomorrow and explain everything."

"Yes, you will." She nodded toward the car.

163

"Shandra cares about you. Don't mess this up."

"What did you two talk about?" He knew Shandra wouldn't say anything to make his mom think they were making wedding plans.

"That I need to back off and not smother you." She pivoted. "This is me not smothering. Call me tomorrow."

Ryan chuckled. Whatever Shandra said had clicked with his mom. He opened the driver's door, pulled the seat forward, and deposited their bags in the back. Sliding behind the wheel, he glanced at Shandra.

She smiled. "Wouldn't have pictured you as a collector of old cars."

"I spent my first pay check to buy this car. It was rare then and even rarer now."

She raised a hand, fluttering the tarp. "Especially with this classic cover."

Ryan shook his head. "I've been saving. I'll have enough to get the cloth top this spring. I usually store this in the barn at Dad's for the winter."

The semi roared to life, black smoke puffing into the air above the stacks. Ryan glanced over. His dad was behind the wheel, pulling the truck out of the middle of the road.

Before the staters and Speaks started the traffic moving, Ryan put the car in gear and headed down the road, passing the long line of cars backed up halfway to Huckleberry.

"You'd think they'd turn around and go home," Shandra said.

"It would make sense." Ryan had relayed all he knew about the accident to the law enforcement but something nagged at his mind. Why had the driver run?

His phone rang. Ryan pulled it out, noticing it was Speaks. "Greer."

"Ryan, there's something strange about the driver," Speaks said.

"What?"

"We contacted the trucking company and this truck was reported stolen in Missoula about five hours ago."

"What is it carrying?" That explained why the driver ran. He was driving a stolen rig.

"That's the weird part. It was empty. And someone ten cars back toward Huckleberry said a man came out of the trees, climbed into the car behind him and that car turned around and headed back to Huckleberry." Speaks voice registered his puzzlement.

"Thanks. Keep me posted." Ryan hung up.

"Was that about the truck?" Shandra asked.

"Yes. The driver ran because it was stolen." Counting back the hours, the truck was stolen about the same time they left the nursing home. He didn't want to think there was a correlation but it was hard to ignore.

"Stolen from where?"

"Missoula." He glanced over at Shandra. Was she having the same thoughts?

"What was it carrying?"

"Nothing."

She shifted in her seat, facing him more. "Someone stole an empty truck?"

"Apparently. And the driver got in a car on the Huckleberry side. It turned around and headed back to Huckleberry." Did he voice his thoughts?

"When was it stolen?"

"About five hours ago." *About the time we left the nursing home.*

"So ten-thirty, eleven. About the time we left Sunnyside." Shandra's reserved tone, revealed she was having the same thoughts.

Chapter Twenty-one

Shandra's chest tightened. Had Melody's niece called someone? It didn't make sense, but the facts couldn't be ignored.

"I think we need to find out more about Melody," she said.

Ryan's jaw clenched. He glanced her way. "I was having the same thoughts."

Knowing Ryan had the same suspicion made her feel they were getting closer to answers about her father's death.

They drove through Huckleberry. Usually the silver Christmas bells hanging from the lamp posts and the Christmas displays in the store windows filled her with happiness. Growing up they had a fake Christmas tree and no other decorations. Her mother didn't like the mess. So living in a community where they did everything they could to promote Christmas sales, she loved the gaudy and the sophisticated decorations.

Today, however, there was too much on her mind to let the holiday cheer into her heart.

"I plan to stay the night and leave early in the morning. If there is someone out there trying to stop you from discovering what happened to your father, I don't want to leave you alone." Ryan reached over and grasped her hand.

"You'll get no argument from me." Having Ryan in the house would make her feel better. But he'd have to go to work tomorrow, and she'd have to deal with the knowledge there could be someone planning to do her harm.

That would mean moving Lil out of the guest room and back to her room in the barn. "What about Lil? We can't leave her out in the barn by herself."

"I'll sleep on the couch. No sense in sending her out to the barn when there could be someone lurking around."

She sensed Ryan wasn't happy to have the older woman in the house with them. And she was of the same mind. She hadn't told Lil of her dreams and Ella. The woman was too grounded to understand.

The car started up her driveway.

The first bit of incline and the tires spun. "Damn!" Ryan smacked the steering wheel with the palm of his hand.

Shandra jumped. She'd not seen this kind of anger in him before. This was what she needed to see before thinking of a future with the man. She'd spent enough of her life in fear of making a man mad.

168

"Sorry. I knew we'd be lucky to get up the drive with the bald tires on this thing. I'll walk up and get your Jeep. You shouldn't be hobbling on that leg." He opened the door.

Shandra nodded and sat in the running car as Ryan jogged up the driveway. Their earlier conversation ran through her head. She reached over, locked the driver's door, and then her own.

The driveway ran through towering pine trees. The day was waning. The bit of sun that had filtered through the trees, faded, turning the world into grays and blacks. The dark didn't usually make Shandra nervous, however, after the day she'd had, she couldn't control the panic chilling her spine and making her glance all around.

She caught the glimpse of something moving through the trees to her right. Reaching over, she pulled the knob that turned on the headlights. The backlight of the headlamps gave her a bit of reprieve from the blackness outside the car.

Her fingers wrapped around her phone. Not sure who she would call if someone leaped out of the woods around her, but it gave her comfort.

Lights bobbed in the road ahead. Her Jeep stopped in front of the Mustang. Ryan stepped out of the driver's door and hurried over to her side. Shandra pulled the lock up and opened the door.

"I'll get you in the Jeep then get our bags and lock this up." Ryan grasped her arm, pulling her up and out of the low car. When she stood, he scooped her up in his arms.

"I can walk. It's just a sprain," she protested.

"Not in this deep snow. You'll just injure it worse." He stopped at the passenger side of the Jeep. "Open the door."

She grabbed the handle and swung the door open.

Ryan placed her on the seat. "Be right back."

He returned to the Mustang, retrieved their bags, turned off the car, and came back to the Jeep.

"You'll have to back all the way to the house. Lil's made tall sides to this road by plowing it," Shandra said, watching Ryan peer into the side view mirror.

"No problem."

He was true to his word. They pulled up in front of the house without him bumping the Jeep into the piles of snow on the side of the road.

All the downstairs lights were on.

"Oh no! Hazel can't get out with your car stuck in the driveway." Where would Hazel sleep?

"When you're settled, I'll use your tractor and pull my car up to the house." Ryan turned the Jeep off.

"Are you going to put the Jeep back in the barn?" Shandra asked. She'd made a promise to herself to take special care of the vehicle when she bought it. The Jeep had to last her many years.

"Yes. When I put the Jeep in the barn, I'll grab the tractor." Ryan stepped out of his side.

Shandra popped the door open and slid to the ground, keeping her weight on her uninjured foot.

Ryan hurried over.

"You're not carrying me into the house. You'll give those two ladies gossip." Shandra allowed Ryan to put an arm under hers to help keep the weight off the foot and hobbled up to the front door.

Hazel opened the door. "My, what happened to you two?"

"Shandra can tell you. I have to use the tractor to get my car out of the driveway so you can go home." Ryan dropped their bags inside the door.

"I better come help you," Lil said, using crutches to swing into the entry.

"You're in no shape to help," Shandra said, putting a hand on Lil's arm. She motioned toward the door. "Go. You have to be as tired as I am. Get your car moved so you can come in and have a hot shower and cocoa."

Ryan pivoted out the door, closing it behind him.

"What happened?" Hazel asked, helping Shandra into the great room.

"A truck jack-knifed right in front of us, and we ended up down an embankment." Shandra eased down onto her couch and sighed. Sheba stood up from her spot in front of the fireplace and placed her head in Shandra's lap. "This is what I need. Thanks, Sheba."

"Who responded to the call?" Hazel asked.

"Deputy Speaks and two state patrol." Shandra felt the chills coming on. "I should be out there helping Ryan." She didn't like the idea of him outside alone.

"He'll be fine. He's a man." Lil stood by the hallway to the kitchen and guest bedroom. "You look like you could use a hot shower. Hazel, why don't you take Shandra on into her shower? I'll start some warm milk for cocoa."

Shandra liked the idea of a hot shower. What she didn't like was leaving Lil alone so she could slip outside.

"I think I'll stay here. The fire and Sheba will warm me up. Lil keep me company while Hazel makes the cocoa."

Lil grudgingly plopped down on the easy chair. Hazel smiled and left the room.

***

Ryan drove the Jeep into the barn, tucking the vehicle in the corner where he'd found it. The tractor and loader sat on the other side of the barn door. A chain was wrapped around the three-point hitch. One less thing to try and find. He climbed up onto the seat and reached down to turn the key. No key.

He pulled out his phone and called Shandra.

"Are you stuck?" she asked.

"Not yet. Where's the key to the tractor?" He hoped it wasn't in the house. Stepping into the warmth again would make it hard to walk back out in the cold.

"It's hanging on a hook in Lil's room. It's to the right of the door."

"Thanks." He pushed the phone back in the case and headed to Lil's room in the barn.

At the door, he heard movement inside. He listened with his ear to the door. There was definitely someone moving around in the room.

He pulled his backup firearm out of the holster in his left boot. He stood to the side, grasped the handle, and shoved the door open.

Chapter Twenty-two

No one shot or ran into the barn.

The room was dark.

"Police. Come out with your hands up," he said loudly.

Nothing.

He didn't like going into a dark room, it brought flashes of walking down the dark alley in Chicago the night he was jumped and beaten to within an inch of life. There had to be a light switch inside the door. His heart raced and sweat moistened his brow and palms. He wiped his gun hand on his pants, wrapped it around the revolver, and used his other hand to swipe the inside wall, feeling for a light.

The light flashed, blinding him with its brightness. He blinked three times and stepped into the doorway.

He scanned the room. Nothing. I know I heard

something in here. There wasn't a closet or other exit in the room. After the day I've had, I probably didn't even hear anything.

Ryan spotted the key on the hook and stepped forward to grab it. Something orange and hissing, leaped off a top shelf and landed on his shoulder before scurrying out of the room.

Lil's cat!

He should have asked about the creature.

The barn doors were wide open.

Damn! He didn't think the animal was allowed out at night. There were too many predators in the woods.

"There's nothing I can do about it now." He left the door to Lil's room open enough for a cat to get through and started up the tractor. Getting his car out of the drive was more important than finding a cat at the moment. If the animal wasn't back in the barn when he put the tractor up, he'd call for it.

The tractor purred to life and he headed down the driveway.

***

Shandra heard the tractor leave and fifteen minutes later it returned. Poor Ryan had to be freezing.

Hazel and Lil sat in the dining area playing cards.

"I heard Ryan come back. I'm going in the kitchen to get some cocoa for him," she said, pushing to her feet. Hazel had found a stretch bandage in the emergency kit and wrapped Shandra's ankle. The support from the bandage made it bearable to put a little weight on it.

Lil stuck out a crutch. "Here, use this."

"Thanks." Shandra found using the crutch helped.

In the kitchen, she poured fresh milk into the small pan she used for warming milk.

Scratching on the window above the sink caught her attention. The glare of the overhead light made it hard to see anything outside. She flipped the light off. A round orange face with shining eyes stared in the window.

Shandra screamed and jumped back, crashing the crutch to the floor.

Ryan burst through the back door at the same time Hazel raced in from the other room.

"What was it?" Ryan asked, pulling her to him.

"An orange..." Her mind recognized what she'd seen. "It was Lewis. Staring in the window."

"I've been trying to find him. He ran out of Lil's room when I got the tractor key." Ryan released her and ran back outside, calling, "Lewis, here kitty, kitty."

He'd left the backdoor open. Lewis ran in the door and through the kitchen.

"Hazel holler at Ryan that Lewis is safe." Shandra couldn't stop the giggle bubbling up. The incident wasn't funny. Giggling settled her nerves.

Hazel called out the back door, "We have Lewis. Come in." She shook her head and wandered back into the other room.

Shandra stifled her giggles and finished making Ryan's cocoa.

The door opened. Ryan and a burst of cold air entered.

Shandra shivered and wrapped her sweater tighter around her.

"The driveway is clear of my car. I hope you don't

mind, I put it in the barn. That tarp top doesn't hold up well under too much snow." Ryan hung up his coat on the rack by the back door and bent to take off his boots.

"That's fine. There's plenty of room." She held out the cup of cocoa when he walked over to her.

"Thanks." He took a sip. "That's good. I'm freezing. Mind of I take this with me to the shower?"

"Go ahead. I knew you'd want to get warmed up."

Ryan glanced at the crutch still on the floor. "Need help?" He picked up the crutch and handed it to her.

"No. Lil lent this to me and it works good." She put the crutch under her arm and headed to the great room. Ryan followed.

"Hazel, the driveway is clear. You can head home whenever you're ready," Ryan said, picking up his duffel bag.

"When I finish this hand of pinochle, I'll head home." She glanced from Ryan to Shandra and back to Ryan. "Unless you want me to leave sooner?"

Ryan laughed. "Hazel, you can spend the night if you want. But I get the couch. You'll have to bunk with Lil or sleep in the easy chair."

Shandra watched the bantering between Ryan and Hazel. How could he joke and laugh when there could be someone lurking outside?

Ryan winked at Shandra and left the room.

She didn't know what to make of any of this. Pulling out a sketch pad, she started writing down everything she knew. Then she began drawing the dreams with Ella in them. There had to be a clue in the dreams.

"Honey? Honey? I'm leaving now."

Shandra glanced up from the sketch she was working on. She'd traveled into the dream as she drew it. Hazel's voice pulled her back to the present.

"Okay. Drive careful." She put her sketch pad to the side and started to stand.

"Don't get up. I know my way out. Thank you for thinking of me. I've enjoyed visiting with Lil." Hazel turned to Lil. "When this snow is gone, you and I will get together for lunch every week."

"It's a date," Lil said, from the easy chair, her foot propped up on a stool.

"Tell Ryan good-night." Hazel pulled the collar of her coat up and headed out the door.

"Good night!" Shandra called as the door closed.

"What you drawing that you didn't hear Hazel talking to you?" Lil asked.

"Just some dreams I had. Nothing important." She closed the sketch pad. "I'm going to take a shower. Ryan should be done by now. Keep him company until I get back." Shandra needed some space from her drawings. Hopefully, when she came back and looked at them, she'd see what she couldn't see right now.

***

Ryan finished his shower, shaved, and put on his lounge pants and T-shirt. He didn't have any slippers with him, so he put on a pair of socks to keep his feet warm. He'd drank all the cocoa and was hoping for another cup when he wandered out to the great room.

He found Lil leafing through what looked like a sketch pad.

"Shandra know your look at her drawings?"

Lil jumped and tossed the sketch pad to the side.

"I'm not looking at her drawings."

Ryan laughed. "I caught you red-handed."

"Just like a cop. Always expectin' everyone to be doin' wrong." Her cheeks reddened in color.

She knew he had her. Ryan sat on the couch on the other side of the sketch pad. "Why were you interested in Shandra's drawings?"

"She said they weren't anything, just drawings of her dreams. But she'd been so absorbed in drawing it that she didn't even hear Hazel when she was telling her good-bye." Lil ran a hand over the sketch book. "It was as if the drawings held her captive."

The hair on the back of Ryan's neck tingled. The dreams did have a hold on Shandra. He just hoped they didn't get her killed. And he hoped Shandra would share her drawings with him. Maybe he could help her sort them out.

"I'm through in the guest bath. You can go to bed if you want." Ryan smiled, hoping his comment didn't sound like he was throwing her out of the great room.

"I can take a hint." Lil pushed up off the couch and hobbled down the hall toward the guest bedroom. "You might want to follow me and get your blankets."

He stood and carried his cup into the kitchen before stepping into the guest bedroom.

"Up there. The top shelf of the closet. Them pile of blankets is for the couch." Lil pointed to the closet in the room. Lewis was curled in a ball on the bed.

Ryan retrieved the bedding.

Back at the couch, he dropped them on one end and returned to the kitchen to make more cocoa.

"You must be starving."

He turned at Shandra's voice. "It's been a while since lunch."

"Let me make you a grilled cheese and soup." Shandra hobbled over to the refrigerator.

"No, you sit. Tell me where things are and I'll make us both a grilled cheese and soup."

"But you're my guest," Shandra protested.

"I'm the only one in the house not injured. Sit." Ryan maneuvered her over to a stool. He returned to the fridge and extracted the items that he needed.

"Do you think that truck tried to run us off the road?"

Her voice was so low, Ryan barely heard her question.

He placed the cheese, bread, and butter on the counter across from Shandra. Keeping his voice low as well, he answered, "I can't rule it out. Though why… as far as I know we haven't any solid proof who murdered your father. And there was no way Melody called in a hit on us. She was too forthcoming with her answers."

"But her niece didn't want us talking to her before she even knew what we were talking about." Shandra picked up a piece of the cheese he'd sliced and nibbled on it.

"I'm going to look into who is paying for Melody's room at the nursing home. That's one of the upper scale places. She couldn't afford that as the widow of a rodeo clown." While he was in the shower, Ryan had made up his mind to look deeper into Melody Dean Harmond.

"Who could the niece have called?" Shandra picked up another piece of cheese. She waved it instead of eating it. "For the truck to have been stolen in

Missoula, I'd bet my money on someone from the M Ranch Rough Stock Company." She shuddered. "It can't be Adam's father, he's dead. That leaves Adam. From what Melody said, they were both in the room at the time of the drawing."

"But what would the older Malcolm have to gain from killing your father?" Ryan had been hashing that over in his mind on the drive from Sunnyside.

"As far as I know, nothing." She sighed heavily. "Adam had a lot to gain. My mother and his pride." She shook her head. "All these years I knew he didn't like me. I thought it was because I was half Nez Perce. But I was a reminder that Mother had bedded an Indian to spite Adam."

Ryan rounded the counter and pulled Shandra into his arms. "Don't let his sick mind change who you are. You've been strong for this long, don't allow his negativity to pull you down." He tipped her face up. "You have grown into a wonderful woman who is embracing your heritage. His hatred of that couldn't stop you."

The sadness left her eyes. Strength and determination stared back at him.

"If he killed my father, we have to find proof."

He kissed the top of her head and returned to the sandwiches. "We will. We just have to gather all the evidence we can and confront him on Saturday."

Chapter Twenty-three

Shandra picked up her sketch pad to make a bed on the couch for Ryan while he cleaned up the dishes. She flipped through the pages. Each dream had to mean something. She understood the first one. Her father's death and that he was too good a rider to fall off Loco on his own. The second dream with the tornado of heads. She still didn't know if Charlie Franks had anything to do with her father's death. Had Coop discovered anything in the tribal records? All the other people in the tornado had something to gain or prove from Father falling off the horse.

And then there was the third dream. Being chased and Ryan saving her. Shandra shook her head. Grandmother wanted her to continue digging and she had faith Ryan would keep her granddaughter from harm.

"What are you looking at?" Ryan asked, walking up behind her.

"Sketches I made of my dreams. It's confusing because there are so many that had, in their minds, a reason to kill him." She closed the pad before Ryan saw the sketch of him saving her.

"Maybe I can decipher their meanings. I'm not as close to them as you are." He held out his hand.

"Let me think about it." She placed the pad on the table and finished making the bed on the couch. "Are you sure you'll be comfortable here?"

"It's warm and soft. I'll be fine." He put an arm around her shoulders. "I checked all the downstairs doors and windows. The house is locked up tight, and I'll be right here."

"I know. I won't worry tonight. But tomorrow when you go to work, I have to go out and feed the horses. I can't hide in the house all the time." She didn't want to sound like a paranoid chicken, but the incident with the truck was still fresh in her mind.

"I'll feed the horses in the morning before I leave, and I'll be back after my shift. I don't feel they'll try anything in the daylight."

"They tried to run us off the road in the daylight," she countered.

"But they bungled it. We're still alive and now know something is up. They'll have to be sneakier. Don't open the door for anyone who drives up here unless you know them." Ryan pulled her into a hug. "Promise?"

"Yes. Thank you for believing in me. I know we haven't found any positive proof of anything, but we will and you can take the information to whoever will prosecute the murderer of my father." Even though, all these years, she knew her father hadn't left her on purpose, it would help her finally put him and her grandmother at peace.

"When we have enough to convict, I'll take all the information to the D.A." He hugged her tight. "It's been a long day."

"Yes, you were trudging around in the cold of hours." She kissed his cheek. "Good night."

He released her. "Good night."

Shandra walked over to her bedroom, opened the door, glanced back at Ryan watching her, and stepped into the room, closing the door against temptation.

***

Ryan woke, dressed, and fed the horses. He did a quick reconnaissance of the area around the buildings to see if there were any new footprints. The snow wasn't disturbed. Returning to the house, he stepped into an olfactory heaven. The spicy scent of yeast and cinnamon and the greasy tang of bacon.

Shandra was busy flipping eggs and rearranging bacon on a cast iron griddle.

"You work that turner like a pro," he said, pouring a cup of coffee.

"One of my part-time jobs in college was a short-order chef." She wrinkled her nose. "I didn't like leaving every shift smelling and feeling like grease."

"Don't you know men prefer bacon perfume?" He grinned and kissed her cheek.

"Not all men."

Her tone made him stare at her. "What man doesn't

like the scent of bacon?"

"It was another lifetime. Never mind." She turned from him and set plates and silverware on the counter.

"There's only two. What about Lil?" Ryan asked, placing his cup by a plate and sitting down.

"She was up before you went outside. She's had breakfast and is working on a puzzle in the other room." Shandra slid over-easy eggs on to his plate. She replaced the pan and plopped three slices of bacon, and a hot gooey cinnamon roll beside the eggs.

"You weren't up making these when I left,' he said, pointing to the cinnamon roll with his fork. The scent from the sweet roll make his mouth water.

"I keep some in the freezer. I pulled them out last night and put them in the refrigerator to thaw overnight. Then I did a quick rise method and you have fresh cinnamon rolls."

Ryan forked a bite into his mouth. The flavors made his tongue sing. "I've never tasted anything this good before." He hadn't. Even his mom and grandmother's cinnamon rolls didn't compare to these.

"Thanks. They are my specialty. I made them for the café where I worked." She put an egg and one slice of bacon on her plate along with a cinnamon roll. Before sitting, she replenished her tea.

"These are insane," Ryan said, ignoring the other food on his plate as he devoured the cinnamon roll.

"Glad you approve." She grinned and put a bite in her mouth.

The talents Shandra had amazed him. His first encounter with her, he would have never guessed her to be so down-to-earth and able to do so many things he'd witnessed in their short relationship.

"Remember, don't open the door today to anyone you don't know. Tell Lil too. She could let someone in when you're in another room." Ryan wasn't about to have anything happen to Shandra. Every day he spent with her, he could see them growing old together when they were ready to commit.

"I already told her to stay inside and not let anyone in. I think I'll put up some Christmas decorations." Shandra's eyes sparkled with excitement.

"No climbing up on things with that ankle," he reprimanded and kissed her cheek to soften his words.

"Not me, Lil."

Ryan started to comment and Shandra burst into laughter.

"You think you're funny." He stabbed his fork into the remaining half of Shandra's cinnamon roll. "You lose this for making fun of me."

Shandra laughed harder.

"What's all the noise in here?" Lil hobbled into the kitchen. "You made cinnamon rolls and didn't tell me." She hobbled to the pan and plopped two rolls onto a plate and stood at the end of the counter eating them with joy on her face.

"See. These things are beyond good. You should market them," Ryan said. He dug into the rest of his breakfast. He still had to get to Warner and grab his work revolver and his work vehicle. He finished the food and put his dishes in the sink.

"Shandra, do you mind if I use your Jeep to get to work. I don't want to chance getting the Mustang stuck trying to get out of here. I'll get here early enough tonight to plow the road and if there isn't any more snow overnight, I can take the Mustang the next day." Ryan plucked another cinnamon roll out of the pan.

"I don't plan to go anywhere today. Go ahead. It makes more sense than taking your car." Shandra barely limped as she placed her dishes in the sink. She crossed to the space on the counter where her keys hung from a rack.

She tossed her keys to Ryan. "It might need gas to get you to Warner."

"I can fill up in Huckleberry." He pulled on his coat then walked over to where Shandra stood. "Thanks. See you tonight." He kissed her cheek and left through the back door.

Shandra stared at the door. Part of her was fluttering with happiness over the way Ryan treated her and the other was worried about being stuck at the house with only a tractor, Ryan's Mustang, and Lil's old pickup for transportation if there was an emergency. Not a one of the vehicles was reliable.

"This is like watching the Brady Bunch," Lil said.

Shandra spun toward Lil. "What do you mean?"

"Ryan kissing you on the cheek as he heads off to work leaving the little housewife behind to tend to family things."

"I'm beginning to think you did something to your head when you broke that leg." Shandra headed out of the kitchen. "Put the dishes in the dishwasher, I have a phone call to make."

In her small office, she picked up her cell phone and dialed Coop's phone number.

"Hey Shandra," he answered.

"Hi Coop. Have you had a chance to do any digging on how Charlie Frank could afford his ranch?" Shandra asked.

"All I could find was that the land had once belonged to Charlie's great-grandfather on his mother's side. It looks like he took over the tribal trust."

"Then his getting that land after my father died is just coincidental." Shandra wasn't sure if that made her happy or upset. She was glad the old man wasn't part of her father's death and it ruled out one person, but at the same time it would have made things easier if he had gotten the property some other way.

"Thanks for looking into it for me."

"You're welcome. I looked up something else. Jessie Lawyer was in a Whiteman's jail three times for harassing your mother. Your mother filed the complaints with the tribal police, but they sent her to jail outside the reservation because they were both non-tribal members." Coop cleared his throat. "You want me to try and talk to her some more about your dad?"

"No. The way she responded the night I talked to her, I think she needs to be talked to by the police. I'll let Ryan know what you found out. Thanks, again." Shandra hung up and thought about it a minute. What would Jessie have to do with her father's death? She seemed to like him. Why would she wish him dead?

Shandra called Ryan.

"Anything wrong?" he asked.

"No. I called my cousin to see what he found out about Charlie Franks. He received his land through his family. Just coincidence about the timing. But Coop did discover that my mom had Jessie Lawyer, the woman who attacked me in the bar, put in jail three times for harassment. She seemed to genuinely like my father, but maybe my mom pushed her too far."

"I'll check into it today," Ryan said.

"Thanks."

"Anytime."

Shandra hung up and headed out of the office. The Christmas decorations were out in the studio. Ryan told her not to go out of the house, but she could go out the back door and in the back door of the studio and haul the boxes over with the toboggan she kept to pull Sheba around.

Chapter Twenty-four

Ryan called dispatch to let them know he was headed home. He'd put in enough overtime to get off a couple hours early. He wanted to plow out Shandra's driveway while there was still light to see. The forecast called for no more snow until next week. Once the driveway was cleared it should stay that way, and he could take his Mustang home. Luckily, the damage to the pickup was fixable. It would be a couple weeks before he could drive the vehicle, but he wouldn't have to go out and buy a new one.

He was positive the driver of the semi had wanted to run them off the road. What he couldn't figure out was how did he know that was Ryan's pickup? He'd never met Shandra's stepfather or mother. How would they know the make and license plate of his vehicle?

Shandra's Jeep crawled through the snow without a

problem. He'd worry less knowing she had a reliable vehicle with the way the snow was piling up this year. Driving out of the trees and into the meadow in front of her house, he couldn't miss the white lights twinkling inside the house even though it was still light outside. He found Shandra's childlike enthusiasm for Christmas catching.

Before pulling the Jeep into the barn, he stopped in front of the house. This was what his soul needed. To come home every night to a house lit up with warmth and love. Shandra hadn't said she loved him, and he hadn't said the words to her, but they were growing closer each time they were together. And this scene made him hope there could be a future between them.

He drove on to the barn. Opening the doors, he noticed the horses chomping away on grain. Someone, most likely Shandra, had been out here treating the horses. And after he'd told her to not go outside.

He parked the Jeep and strode to the house. He'd have a discussion with Shandra before clearing the road.

He tried the back door and the knob turned easily in his hand. She was supposed to keep the door locked. Didn't this woman ever obey when it came to her life?

Shandra stood on a chair in the great room attaching a garland across the wide stone chimney of the fireplace.

"What are you doing?" he asked.

She started and wobbled on the chair. Ryan rushed across the room to catch her if she fell.

"I'm hanging a garland," Shandra said when she'd caught her balance. "What are you doing back so early?"

"Obviously, catching you doing things you were told not to." He grabbed her around the waist and set her on the floor. "I told you to stay inside, keep the doors locked, and don't climb around." He waved his hand to encompass the room, "You've done none of the things I asked you to do for your safety."

She rammed her hands on her hips. "If I was going to decorate I had to get the decorations. I went out the back door and into the back door of the studio. I used the toboggan to pull the boxes and I locked the door behind me." She pointed to the garland. "As for the garland, well, I figure climbing up on one chair couldn't put me in too much danger."

Ryan shook his head. "The horses are eating grain and the back door was unlocked when I came in." The stunned expression on Shandra's face told him she hadn't been the one to do those things.

"Lil!" they said in unison.

The woman was wrapped in a large purple robe as she hobbled into the room. "What you both calling me for?"

Shandra walked forward. "Did you go to the barn?"

"Yes. I missed my robe. It's cold sitting around in here if I'm not next to the fireplace." Lil stuck her chin up as if defying Shandra to say something.

"And you stopped to give the horses grain," Ryan said.

"Well, I give them some every day and figured you wouldn't think of it." She nodded her head once as if affirming her own comment.

"But I told you, we had to stay in the house and

keep the doors locked," Shandra said in a tone that reflected she was talking to a child.

"You went out and got your Christmas doodads so I figured I could get something to keep me warm." She sounded like a child defending her actions.

Ryan ran a hand across the back of his neck. "You both need to stay in the house until we can get a line on the guy who ran us off the road."

A jazz tune erupted from Shandra's phone sitting on the dining room table.

Shandra walked to the table and picked up the phone. *Mother*. She glanced at Ryan and decided right now she'd rather deal with her mother.

"Hello Mother," she answered.

"Shandra are you still coming to the dinner Saturday night?" her mother asked, without so much as a hello.

"Yes. We're still planning on coming." She held the phone out a bit when Ryan stepped next to her to listen.

"Good. Your charming Mr. Pickley means a lot to Adam. I don't want to disappoint him."

Shandra glanced at Ryan. He shook his head. If her mother only knew they were coming early and Mr. Pickley and Adam were going to be disappointed when they left early.

"I hope Adam wouldn't do anything illegal to get Mr. Pickley's contract." Shandra said.

Ryan bumped her with his shoulder. His eyes narrowed and he shook his head.

She must have said too much or something she shouldn't have said.

"Adam only does what he must to get what he

wants. See you Saturday."

Silence. "Did you hear that last part? The one about Adam always gets what he wants?" Shandra said as a shiver raced down her spine.

"I heard it. You shouldn't antagonize them. They may figure out we know what they're up to." Ryan said. He pivoted to the kitchen. "I'm headed to clean the drive. I want to get it done before it gets dark." He peered straight in her eyes. "That's why I'm here early."

Shandra smiled. "Not because you were checking up on us?"

He shook his head and left the room and the house.

Shandra stared at the phone in her hand. Why had mother called to confirm Saturday? Is she that nervous about making Adam happy? Or is she making sure we're coming for another reason?

"What's that about? You look like you ate a sour pickle," Lil said, sitting down on the couch.

"That's how I feel," she replied and wandered into the kitchen to see what she could whip up for their dinner.

***

Saturday morning, Shandra was up making waffles for breakfast when Ryan came in from feeding the horses.

"Smells delicious in here." He left his coat and boots by the back door and poured a cup of coffee.

Having Ryan spend the night all week, even with Lil in the house, had been a pleasant experience. She enjoyed making his breakfast in the morning while he did the chores.

"I bet you'll be ready to get Lil back to her room in

the barn so you can sleep on a bed instead of that couch," Shandra said, seeing him twist his torso.

"I don't want to kick her out when we still haven't a lead on who ran us off the road, but I did get an interesting call while I was out in the barn." He sipped his coffee.

"Just a minute, let me get this last waffle out." Shandra placed the last waffle on a plate and placed them in front of Ryan. She filled her cup with tea from a pot and sat next to him at the counter.

"Okay, what was your interesting call?" Shandra started buttering her waffle.

"I said I would find out more about Melody Dean Harmond?"

"Yes." Shandra stopped buttering to pay close attention to what Ryan had to say.

"I said that was a pricey nursing home. Her monthly payment is being paid by M Ranch Rough Stock Company." He raised an eyebrow.

"Adam? It has to be because he knows she knows what he did?" Shandra shoved her plate to the middle of the counter. "Do you think it's blackmail? I mean, really I can't see Melody blackmailing him. But why would he pay for her nursing home?"

"You're correct about the blackmail. But it isn't Melody. It's her niece."

"The one who threw us out of the room?" This was making more sense. Melody, during one of her more lucid days, like when they visited her, must have mentioned the events of the day Edward Higheagle died and how it had been improper protocol. Perhaps the niece decided to get money for her aunt with the information.

"Yes. When a deputy I sent to the nursing home talked with the manager, she said Marsha Smith secured the room with her money and said the rest would be coming from the M Ranch Rough Stock Company." Ryan pushed her plate back in front of her. "Looks like we have one more question to ask your stepfather today."

Shandra had trouble swallowing her sip of tea. She could already feel the tension building in her shoulders and neck. The feeling she lived with most of her life in Adam Malcolm's home.

Chapter Twenty-five

Shandra sat in the passenger seat of her Jeep as Ryan drove up the winding paved road that led them onto the M Ranch. Once she'd turned eighteen, she rarely came here. She couldn't even call it home. It had never felt like home to her. She had felt like an outsider here for fourteen years.

Ryan reached over, grasped her hand, and squeezed. "I'm here."

She smiled. "I know. I wouldn't have agreed to this visit if you hadn't been able to come with me." She glanced at him. "But arriving now instead of for the dinner will send Mother into a tizzy along with the questions we're going to ask..." She wrapped her free hand and arm around her middle. "My stomach is tied in knots."

"They can't do anything to you. You're an adult

and you have a lawman with you. They'd be stupid to try anything." He parked the Jeep at the front walk that lead to the porch that spanned the length of the centuries-old, log house. It reminded Shandra of lodges she'd seen in magazines.

"Come on." Ryan climbed out his side and came around to open her door. "I'm here," he repeated and took her hand. Leading her up the steps.

She didn't know why her knees were jelly. Maybe because she'd always felt something was off between her and Adam, and knowing it could be because he killed her father, she wasn't sure if she could control her emotions.

They walked up the steps and Ryan grasped the large, brass ring in the bull-head knocker. He whacked it three times and grinned at her.

The door opened and Agnes, the housekeeper who'd spent more time with Shandra than her mother, stared at her. "Shandra, you were to come for the party, not now."

"I don't plan to stay for the party. Are mother and Adam around? I'd like to speak to them." Seeing the one friendly face had bolstered her courage.

"Yes. Your mother is finishing the decorating in the great room, and your stepfather is in his office."

"Agnes? Agnes, who's here?" Mother called.

Her mother emerged from the great room into the entryway. Her eyes narrowed and her mouth pursed. "What are you doing here so early?" She plucked at Shandra's coat and tsked at her blue jeans. "And not even dressed for a party."

"We aren't here for the party. We have some things

we would like to ask you and Mr. Malcolm," Ryan said.

"Questions? You? We've never met you before. I don't understand." Then her eyes lit up. "Oh, you want to ask Adam." She smiled. "Take off your coats. Agnes! Agnes, bring some hot tea into the study, please."

Shandra wasn't sure why her mother was so cooperative, but she'd go with it. She handed her coat over, as did Ryan.

"Come along. Adam will be so happy to hear this," Shandra's mother said, leading them down the hall to the one room in the house Shandra had been forbidden to enter. Ever.

Mother opened the door wide. "Adam, look who's here, and they have a question for you."

Adam looked up from the paperwork on his desk. The look of disbelief didn't get wiped away fast enough. When he caught himself, his look turned to disdain.

"I thought you were coming to the party tonight. Your mother specifically asked you if you were coming and you said yes." His deep gruff voice started Shandra's body moving backwards.

Ryan's hand pressed against the small of her back. His strength would get her through this.

"Mr. Malcolm, we have several questions we'd like to ask you pertaining to Shandra's father," Ryan started.

"Her father? Why would I know anything about her father?" He sat back down and stared imperiously at them.

"Her father?" Her mother shrilled. "I thought you were going to ask—"

"I met Phil Seeton." Shandra cut off her mother.

"That old drunk. You can't believe a word he says," Adam huffed.

"That's true. He was a drunk," her mother piped in as she took a stand behind Adam and placed her hands on his shoulders.

Shandra had known deep down her mother would side with Adam, but it still hurt to see her striking such a pose of solidarity with the man.

"He told me there was no way Father should have fallen off that horse. He said Loco wasn't good at bucking, but he was known to stomp a rider when he was down." Shandra watched the pair. Neither one flinched. "The autopsy said Father had benzodiazepine in his system, and someone told the coroner that Father had fallen off a horse and was taking them." She stared at her mother. "Were you the one who told the coroner that Father was taking painkillers?"

Her mother looked perplexed. "No, I didn't talk to anyone. As soon as they said he was dead, I hurried to your Aunt Jo's to get you, and then I went to our house and packed everything up and begged my father to let me stay with them until I figured out what to do."

"So the police never contacted you about your husband?" Ryan asked.

"Never."

Shandra stared at Adam. "Did you say he was on painkillers?"

"No, but that explains why he didn't ride that horse very well." Adam's expression was thoughtful.

"Why did you make sure Father rode Loco?" Shandra asked.

His body stiffened, and his face wrinkled into the

glower he gave her more times than not while she'd lived here. "Are you insinuating I manipulated that ride?"

"Yes. We talked with Melody Dean. She says that day both you and your father were drawing the animals for the day. Which was unusual. Why were you in there?" Shandra asked.

"My dad wanted me to start stepping up and taking over his roles at the rodeos. I was there to learn how the process worked." Adam stared at her, his blue eyes never flinching.

"Ms. Dean said after the president, your father, and you left the room, there was one of the horse's names on a slip of paper on the floor. Like it had been tossed and another name put in its place." Ryan remained at her back.

His statement made her mother's eyebrows raise and Adam's lower, forming a scowl on his face.

"All I can add is, I didn't think Loco was to be used for that round. It was the final round. We usually used the rankest stock for the last day when the money was on the line." His gaze touched on Shandra's face. "You're correct. He wasn't a good bucker. That's why I was surprised his name had come up."

"Who picked the horse for Shandra's father? You or your father?" Ryan asked.

Shandra felt every nerve in her body tighten.

Adam didn't even hesitate. "My dad. After he picked it, he made the comment, 'Let's see that Injun make money with that horse.'" Adam patted her mother's hand resting on his shoulder. "I didn't think too much of it at the time. My father didn't think Native

Americans should compete in rodeos."

"And you took a similar view, didn't you?" Shandra said, not keeping her disgust out of her comment. "Only you felt we shouldn't be allowed to do anything that a Whiteman did."

Adam's face reddened.

She couldn't stop the years of hurt and anger that poured forth the words. "How did it make you feel when you realized your princess had slept with an Indian? And had become pregnant? Did you plan out the best way to get rid of him? A way that kept your hands clean?" Shandra started shaking.

Her mother gasped, and Adam's face turned scarlet as his cheeks puffed out in fury.

Ryan placed his hands on her shoulders. "Calm down," he whispered in her ear.

"Mr. Malcolm, I'd like to know why, if your father is the one who switched the horses on Edward Higheagle, that the M Ranch Rough Stock Company is paying for Melody Dean's nursing home and why a semi-truck ran us off the road after visiting with her earlier in the week?"

Ryan's calm questions and his hands on her shoulders, calmed Shandra. She knew an outburst would get her nowhere, but it felt good to get the anger out.

Adam ran a hand over his face.

Her mother backed away from Adam.

"Did you have something to do with Edward's death? You knew I was in the process of getting a divorce. You didn't have to…" her voice faded as Adam stood and walked toward her.

"I swear I had nothing to do with Edward's death. But Melody's niece came to me six months ago with the story that Melody said the ride that killed Edward Higheagle was fixed. The niece said if I didn't pay for the nursing home, she'd tell the rodeo association we'd fixed a ride where a rider was killed. That would ruin everything my family has built. I couldn't let her do that, so I figured it was an investment. When she told me the story, I realized what my dad had done. But I swear—" he faced Ryan and stared him straight in the eye, "—I know nothing about the painkillers. But that would make sense of why the best bronc rider fell off the worst bucking horse."

Shandra watched her stepfather closely. She'd learned to read when he was telling a lie from hearing what he'd tell her mother after he'd told someone what they wanted to hear but wasn't the truth. He wasn't tapping his fingers on his left thigh. He was telling the truth. His dad was the one who switched the horses. But what about the painkillers and the man who tried to run them off the road?

"Do you think your father would have gone as far as to pay someone to drug my father? Did Melody's niece call you after we left the nursing home?" Shandra needed more answers.

Adam shook his head. "I don't think my dad wanted Edward hurt, just knock him down a peg in the standings. And if you think I sent someone to run you off the road, you are wrong. I didn't receive any calls from Melody's niece." He put an arm around her mother and peered into her face. "I'll admit, I've not treated you as fair as I should and did feel jealous every time I looked at you. I wanted to have children with your mother, but she had such a rough delivery with you, it wasn't a chance I could take."

Shandra knew to be the bigger of the two or three she should accept his apology. But at the moment she wasn't ready.

Ryan must have sensed it. "We'll be going now. Thank you for your answers." He grasped her hand and led her out of the room.

"Shandra, wait!" her mother called.

She was torn. It was her mother, but she'd sided every day of Shandra's life with Adam. A man who had just admitted he'd been unkind and jealous of her.

"I'm not coming back for your dinner." Shandra glanced at Ryan. "I won't be back until I know the truth and I can accept the way you've treated me." She squeezed Ryan's hand. "I have found the place I wish to live, surrounded by people who care about me. Goodbye, Mother." Shandra walked out the door and her heart felt lighter than it had in twenty-nine years.

Ryan opened the door of the Jeep. Once she was seated, he leaned in. "Are you sure this is how you want to leave things? The way you said good-bye it sounded like you won't be back or talk to them."

"I'm not sure how I feel about the two of them right now. But saying good-bye after hearing all that, I feel free." She put a hand on his arm. "I'm sorry you were dragged into my dysfunctional family life."

"I'm not. I wondered how you had become such a strong woman. Now I know." He kissed her cheek and closed the door.

A premonition this was the start of a new life for

her, made her giddy inside. But there were still so many unanswered questions.

Chapter Twenty-six

Ryan pulled out of the Malcolm Ranch with his mind spinning. The dead Walter Malcolm was the one who switched up the horses. But not to hurt Edward Higheagle, to discredit him. And he believed Adam when he said he didn't do it or know of the painkillers. Shandra's mother had looked stunned.

"Did your aunt say anything about your mother picking you up the day your father died?" There was something missing. A piece that he couldn't quite wrap his mind around.

"No. Do you want me to ask her?" Shandra twisted in the seat.

He liked when she did this, giving him her full attention as he drove. "Yes. We need to see if your mother's story stands, and then we need to figure out who hated your father enough to slip him the painkillers."

"Why is it important to discover what my mother did?"

"We have to establish who said your father took painkillers. If it wasn't your mother we need to know who. I'm going to request all the records on the case, including the coroner's report. There has to be a note somewhere that states who gave that false information to the coroner or the police."

"And that person would be the one who gave him the pills." Shandra nodded her head.

Ryan liked her quick mind. "Yes. Only the person who was covering up for their part in the murder would have given the false information."

"What about what Melody said about Dicky hitting her for saying they should tell someone about the improper procedure that day?"

"I've been thinking about that. You said Edward beat up Dicky for knocking your mother around. Was Dicky working that rodeo?" Ryan asked.

Shandra shrugged. "I'm not sure, but I have all the information about all the participants, even the volunteers. I can look it up when we get home."

"Call your aunt and ask about your mother. When you're done, I'll pull over at the next wide spot. You can drive while I make phone calls to get the process in motion to get all the records we need."

Shandra dug in her purse for her phone. She punched a number and held it to her ear. "Aunt Jo? This is Shandra." She listened. "Yes, I'm fine. I need to know when Mother picked me up the day Father died."

Ryan glanced over. Her brows were furrowed, and

she tapped her chin with her left pointer finger.

"I see. So she didn't arrive at your house until after the police had called and told you about Father." She listened. "And Mother didn't even know he was dead? If she had been at the rodeo she would have known." Shandra nodded. "Thank you."

She glanced over at Ryan. "Yes, it's a big help."

"No," she shook her head, "we don't know anything yet."

"Yes, I'll let you know what I discover. Bye." Shandra tapped the off button on her phone and peered at him.

Ryan caught a glimpse of what looked like revulsion on Shandra's face before she faced him.

"My mother wasn't even at the rodeo when my father died." She paused, inhaled, and then exhaled. "There is only one place she could have been and that was in someone else's bed."

"Don't jump to conclusions—" Ryan tried to slow down her accusations of her mother.

"I'm not jumping. Once Adam put in his appearance to match the riders and the stock, he wouldn't have to be there the rest of the day. I bet that's why they didn't know all the facts about the 'accident.'" Shandra wiped her coat sleeve across her eyes. "She was sleeping with Adam while my father was…" She snapped her head toward the window and peered out.

Ryan passed two wide spots waiting for Shandra to pull herself together. She was jumping to conclusions, but he had to admit with all they knew, there was a pretty good chance her conclusion was accurate.

When she turned her attention to the road in front of the Jeep, Ryan found a wide spot and pulled over. "Ready to take the wheel?" he asked.

She nodded.

The roads from here to Missoula were snowy enough that he didn't want to be distracted while he drove. Talking to his family, even in an official capacity would still be distracting. He stepped out of the Jeep and walked around to the passenger side. Shandra was already out and passing him. Ryan reached out, grasping her arm, and pulling her to him. "You are your father's daughter. You're strong, determined, and talented. Don't let your mother's actions take any of that away from you."

She kept her gaze trained on his hand on her arm. "Once this is over, I'll have a talk with my mother. But I'm pretty sure, what she'll tell me and what I'll say to her."

Ryan raised an eyebrow. "What will you say to her?"

"You chose your life, and now I'll choose mine." She stared up into his eyes.

He saw strength and determination. "That's what I like to see."

Ryan leaned over and kissed her lips. He knew he had to take things slow with her, but this was a moment that screamed in his head to kiss her.

"What was that for?" Shandra asked, her eyes finally looking sharp and alive.

Since the realization her mother could have been unfaithful the day her father died, there had been a veil of sadness in them.

"For being a strong, independent woman that makes me happy to know." He released her and climbed into the passenger side.

Shandra smiled, shook her head, and rounded the front of the Jeep. Once she was behind the wheel and they were back on the road, Ryan pulled out his phone and started calling in favors.

The first call went to his sister Cathleen at the dispatch desk of the Wieppe County Sheriff's Office.

"Hey, little brother. I heard you've been spending time with Shandra," Cathleen said upon answering his call.

"I still am. I need you to help me get copies of a rodeo accident that happened…" he glanced over at Shandra. "What date did the accident happen?"

"June fifteenth, nineteen eighty-one at two-forty-two p.m. at the Western Stampede Rodeo in Dayton County, Washington."

Ryan knew Shandra had been obsessed with her father's death but knowing all the information off the top of her head, confirmed her obsession. He repeated the information to Cathleen.

"That's a long time ago. Was this a homicide?" Cathleen asked.

"It was recorded as an accident, but we have reason to believe it was murder."

"We? As in another officer?"

He cringed. He was asking Cathleen to put her neck on the line to get him information he should be going through the proper channels to get. "Shandra has reason to believe, and I also have reason to believe, after speaking to people involved, that her father's death wasn't an accident."

"You're supposed to pass cold crimes over—"

"When I investigated the skeleton she dug up that was a cold crime, no one made me pass it off." He sighed. "Sis, a crime is a crime, whether it happened today or thirty years ago. I have knowledge that someone else wouldn't call relevant. But putting it together with what we do know, it is looking more and more like someone murdered Edward Higheagle."

"Okay. You sure you shouldn't have become a lawyer?" She chuckled.

"No way. I don't like wearing a suit. Thanks. Send me the copies when you get them. I'm especially interested in who was interviewed and gave the statement Edward was taking painkillers."

"It may take a couple days. Hey! You could bring Shandra to Christmas Eve dinner and Mass," Cathleen suggested.

"We'll talk about that later. Thanks." Ryan hung up on his sister and turned his attention to Shandra.

She glanced over at him. "Were you able to convince her to help us?" Her gaze went back to the road.

"Yes. But it could take a couple days to get the information."

"I know. We're asking a lot of your sister. Will she get in trouble?"

"Only if the Sheriff finds out." Since he was hired as the Weippe County Detective, Cathleen had dug up information for him many times. Most of the time it was per protocol, but there had been many times that he'd asked her to dig up something based on his gut.

The lawyers didn't like gut instinct to try and win cases on. They wanted facts and all the i's dotted and t's crossed in the reports. They tended to not like to work with police who didn't make them a clean case.

Shandra rolled her head and shook out her shoulders as she drove into Missoula. Ryan had made three more calls and appeared to have made all he'd planned. She hadn't slept well the night before dreading this trip. Now that it was over, she was having trouble staying awake. Even with the anger simmering in her stomach about her mother.

"You'll need to take over if you've finished your calls." She pulled the Jeep into a coffee shop on the outskirts of the city.

"I'm done. Why didn't you tell me you were tired? I could have waited to call until we stopped here." Ryan exited the Jeep and met her at the driver's side.

"I thought I could do it." She accepted his hand as he led her into the coffee shop.

They sat in a booth and ordered a late lunch.

"What I don't understand," Shandra said, "is if Adam didn't send someone to run us off the road after we talked to Melody, who did?"

"Maybe the person with the most to lose if this is all brought out in the open."

Shandra peered into Ryan's eyes. "The niece? Because Melody most likely doesn't know that M Ranch Rough Stock Company is paying for her nursing home."

"I had Cathleen look her up right after we met. I had a feeling she was being too defensive." Ryan pulled out his phone. "Cathleen forwarded the files to my phone." He skimmed through messages. "Marsha isn't Melody's niece. She was a Harmond before she married. She is Dicky's illegitimate daughter. I wouldn't be surprised if Dicky told her to use Melody to get some money out of M Ranch Rough Stock Company."

"But if Adam is paying the nursing home, how could the niece get the money?" Shandra asked.

Ryan scrolled some more, read, and looked up. "The niece works in the billing department of the nursing home. She is charging Adam twice the room rate. I'm not sure how she's getting the rest. I'll send a request to the D.A. in that county to look into the nursing home's records."

Shandra took a sip of her hot tea and peered over the cup at Ryan. "She could have sent someone to run us off the road."

Ryan nodded. "I have a feeling she has more of her daddy's genes in her than Melody knows about."

Worry shot through Shandra. "Do you think she'll harm Melody?"

"No. The longer she stays alive the more money Marsha will get. I think Melody is safe. Unless Adam tells her to go fly a kite now that we know about his father's part in the horse selection that day."

Shandra's heart thudded in her chest. Melody had been hurt enough by the Harmonds. She didn't want her actions to bring her more harm. "I should call Adam and tell him not to say or do anything until we discover who gave Father the painkillers."

"That's a good idea." Ryan leaned back as the waitress placed their orders in front of them.

Shandra pulled out her phone but had to steel herself to actually make the call. She'd been cold to her mother when they left, but now that she knew her mother wasn't even at the rodeo that day... She wasn't certain she could be civil to the woman who gave her life.

But an innocent woman's life depended on this call. She inhaled, released the air, and pushed her mother's number. She'd be nice for now. After this was over—her mother would have a lot of explaining to do.

"Shandra, I'm so glad you—"

"I'm not calling to recant what I said," she interrupted. "You have to make sure Adam doesn't call Marsha Smith and tell her he's no longer paying for Melody Dean's nursing home. I'm afraid if he does, she'd hurt Melody. He needs to wait until we discover who drugged Father before he can stop paying. Please make sure he waits."

"I'll tell him. Melody was a nice person. I'll make sure."

"Thank you. I have to go." Shandra hung up before her mother could say any more.

Ryan watched her over the burger he bit into.

"She said she'll make sure he doesn't say anything. She liked Melody." With that fear off her mind, Shandra dug into her cheeseburger and fries with more gusto and appetite than she thought possible given her internal turmoil.

"I have a feeling you'll be sleeping the rest of the way home." Ryan said, his eyes twinkling.

"I think you may be right. Some of the worries on my mind are gone, others are at bay for the moment, and my stomach is full." Shandra slid the empty basket to the middle of the table and finished her tea.

"When we get back to my place, maybe we should go over the list of people who have been showing up in my dreams and see if we can't narrow down the suspects." Shandra said, standing.

"That's a good idea. Then we'll match that with the information Cathleen comes up with."

"While we're in Missoula, I have a couple questions for Phil," Shandra said as they exited the café.

"Next stop, the retirement home." Ryan held the door for Shandra as she climbed into the Jeep.

She glanced in her mirror and a shiver raced up her spine. The car parked behind them in the parking lot looked like one that had followed them on the freeway into Missoula.

Ryan started up the Jeep.

"Keep an eye on that Chevy behind us. I saw it several times while driving," she said.

"There isn't anyone in the car," Ryan replied.

"If you do see it behind us. We shouldn't go see Phil. I don't want to get him mixed up in this." She would never be able to live with herself if Phil was hurt from her digging up the truth behind her father's death.

Ryan pulled out of the parking lot and headed down the main street. He turned two streets early for the retirement home. "I don't see that car following," he said and continued to the retirement home.

In the parking lot of the retirement home, Shandra scanned the cars that drove by and didn't see the gray Chevy.

They entered the lobby.

The receptionist looked up and smiled. "No dog today?" she asked.

"No, this was a spur of the moment decision to visit Phil," Shandra said, heading down the corridor.

The nurse caught up to her. "Phil has been moved. He's on the other side. Where our residents go when they are having medical issues." Her brown eyes softened with sadness.

"How bad is he?" Shandra asked.

"He's on oxygen and his heart is giving out." She smiled weakly. "But you'll brighten his day. He's in room one-seventy."

"Thank you." Shandra sought Ryan's hand. He'd been her anchor all day.

Hand in hand, they walked through the swinging double doors into the other side of the retirement home. Over here she could feel the despair.

They encountered several helpful nurses and soon stood at the door of one-seventy.

Ryan squeezed her hand, and she walked into the room.

Phil lay in a regular hospital bed. A machine to his left beeped and an oxygen tube protruded from his nose. This was the first time she'd seen him in a hospital gown and not his western attire. He appeared a faded representation of the former rodeo bronc rider and announcer.

"Mr. Seeton? Phil? It's Shandra Higheagle." She released Ryan's hand and captured one of Phil's boney hands in between her two hands. His fingers were cold.

His eyelids fluttered up. He smiled. "I didn't expect

to see you before I went," he said in a whisper.

"I came to ask you a couple more questions, but I don't want to bother you." She smiled even though her chest was constricting with sorrow. Now that she had reconnected with her father's family she had a connection to him, but Phil had given her the strength and courage to discover the truth behind her father's death. He'd become a special person in her heart.

"There isn't much time for me to answer them." He inhaled oxygen. "What are the questions?"

Ryan stepped forward, allowing her to cling to the man.

"We've discovered that the horse Edward Higheagle rode had been manipulated. Walter Malcolm had switched the horse, wanting Higheagle to not be in the money at the rodeo. What we need to know is; how soon before the rodeo starts are the riders and animals announced?"

"They drew names in the morning and posted the list as soon as it was typed up." Phil sucked in more oxygen. "Walter was always saying things against the Indians."

"Do you remember if Dicky Harmond was there that day?" Ryan asked.

"Can't remember. But he was at most of the rodeos on that circuit." Phil drew in more oxygen and started coughing.

Shandra grabbed the tissues and handed them to him. He nodded and pointed to the cup of water with a straw. Shandra helped him get a drink.

"What about Jessie? Was she there?" She was another who had a grudge against her father. Dicky might have had it in for her father, but they say poison is a woman's murder weapon. Painkillers would have been the same difference in this case.

"Jessie was always at the rodeos on that circuit. Either as a barrel racer or a buckle bunny." Phil's watery, faded blue eyes looked into hers. "I'd put my money on Dicky, but he'd have needed someone to get whatever he gave Edward into him. Your father wouldn't have accepted a thing from Dicky."

Shandra had an idea. "Phil, you were there that day. What about my mother and Adam Malcom? Were they there?" Shandra asked. It was a long time ago to ask him about people who wouldn't have been participating in the rodeo.

Phil stared up at the ceiling for a long time. "I'm not sure about Adam, but now that you mention it, they couldn't find your mother when Edward was pronounced dead."

Shandra tamped down the rage swirling in her stomach.

"Did the police question you?" Ryan asked.

"No. They only talked to the men running the chutes and the officials. I don't think they talked to a single cowboy." Phil inhaled more oxygen.

"What about cowgirls? Any of them?" Shandra asked, wondering if Jessie had talked to the police.

"Can't remember." Phil closed his eyes. "I'm mighty tired. It was good seeing you. I'm happy to be going to see my angel. I've missed her since she left me."

Shandra patted his hand. "I wish I would have known about you sooner. Thank you for being a good friend to my father."

"I'll give him your love when I see him." Phil smiled and took a long drag on his oxygen.

"Thank you." Shandra leaned down and kissed his dry, white cheek.

Ryan tugged on her sleeve, and she slowly backed away from Phil.

Out in the hall, she wrapped her arms around Ryan and held on. She'd only known Phil a short time, but he'd left a mark on her heart and helped her to realize what kind of a man her father was.

Ryan hugged her and moved to her side. With one arm still around her shoulders, they left the retirement home.

The grey Chevy was parked three cars over from her Jeep.

Chapter Twenty-seven

"Ryan, look. There's that gray Chevy. You can't tell me this is a coincidence." She rested her head on his arm as if they were having an intimate conversation. She didn't want the person to know they suspected him.

"It isn't a coincidence. It's the same license plate." Ryan kissed the top of her head. "I'm going to put you in the passenger side. Slide over and start the Jeep and drive it in front of the car so he can't drive away. I'll sneak up behind him." Ryan opened the passenger side.

"Be careful," Shandra whispered and crawled in the Jeep, moving over into the driver's seat. She tweaked her ankle a bit maneuvering into position, but she turned the ignition and drove forward, cranking the steering wheel and stopping in front of the car.

She didn't recognize the man behind the wheel.

He started his car.

Ryan jerked open the driver's door and pulled the man out by the collar of his jacket. With efficiency, Ryan splayed the man out over the hood of the gray car and frisked him. Ryan placed a small revolver on the top of the car, out of the man's reach.

She could see they had a running dialog going on the whole time. Ryan shook his head and put cuffs on the man. While the man remained bent over the hood with his hands cuffed behind his back, Ryan pulled out his phone.

Shandra wanted to ask the man questions. But this wasn't Ryan's jurisdiction, and she could get him in trouble more than when he was working with people he knew.

Within minutes the shrill scream of sirens grew closer.

Two city police cars pulled into the parking lot and stopped beside her Jeep. She thought it was overkill to send two cars with four people to pick up someone who was already apprehended.

Once the man was in the back of a police car, Ryan walked over to the Jeep and motioned for her to join him.

She stepped up to his side acknowledging the young and older officer talking to Ryan.

"When did you first notice this man following you?" the older officer asked. His name tag said Sgt. Quinn.

"Shandra noticed him first," Ryan said.

Sgt. Quinn transferred his fuzzy gray eyebrows her direction. "When did you notice the suspect?"

"When we were on I-90 headed west to Missoula. I

noticed because even when I slowed down, the car stayed behind me unlike all the other cars that passed. If I sped up, the gray car would stay with one car between us. Then it was at the restaurant parking lot on the edge of town." She glanced at Ryan.

"That's when she mentioned it to me, and I memorized the license plate." Ryan put an arm around her shoulders.

"Then you came out to get in your vehicle and found him waiting?" Sgt. Quinn asked.

"Yes." They both answered.

"Why do you think this—" the sergeant looked at a driver's license.

Shandra could see it was a Washington driver's license just like the car license.

"Jack Jamison was following you?" The sergeant finished.

Shandra studied Ryan. What would he say?

"I don't know who he is, but I would like to know why he was following us." Ryan said, his anger at the man stalking them evident in his tone.

"Did you ask him what he does for a living?" Shandra asked, watching both Ryan and the sergeant.

"According to this piece of paper, he's a private detective," Sergeant Quinn said.

"Who's he working for?" Shandra and Ryan said in unison.

If they knew who he worked for, she'd bet her best cowgirl boots they'd find out who killed her father.

"I'll take him to the station and see if I can learn anything. What kind of charges do you want to stick him with?" Sgt. Quinn asked.

"Tell him we'll drop the stalking charges if he tells you who he's working for. Then call me." Ryan held out a business card.

Sgt. Quinn nodded. "Pleasure doing business with you, detective."

Ryan hustled Shandra into the passenger side of her Jeep, and he slid in behind the steering wheel.

Once they were pulling out of the parking lot, Shandra shifted to watch Ryan. "Did he say anything when you grabbed him? You two looked like you were doing a lot of talking."

"He was trying to tell me he was going to call the cops on me for harassment. I told him go ahead, but I could save him the time since I was the police." He shook his head. "He didn't say he was a private detective or spill anything to me. Not even his name." Ryan glanced over. "But with his driver's license and car tags being Washington, we can bet our trouble is coming from there."

"That's what I thought. The only person there I can think of is Jessie." Shandra had felt sorry for the woman when she'd tried to get information out of her. But if the woman was having them followed and sent someone to run them off the road…she no longer felt sorry for her.

"We need the records from the accident before we can try to get her to slip up about that day." Ryan maneuvered the Jeep back onto I-90.

"I still want to take a shot at looking at the drawings I made of my dreams." Shandra yawned.

"Go ahead and sleep. I don't think we'll run into any more trouble before I get you back to your place."

Ryan reached across the space between them and brushed the backs of his fingers across her cheek. "Go to sleep. You're safe."

She smiled, closed her eyes, and drifted to sleep to the rumble of the tires on the pavement.

Ella swirled in the air. Her hair stood out like the ghost of Christmas past in the Charles Dickens story. "Ella, you're scaring me," Shandra said, standing below her grandmother. The tornado started, this time it picked Shandra up, swirling her into the gray funnel. She whirled around and around. She grasped at whatever passed her hands. She yanked and found her dead father. She whimpered. "Ella, please. I'm trying." The twister turned faster. Panic froze her body. She found staying still, the tornado didn't carry her where she didn't want to go. If she remained calm, she could see the others tumbling around her. Mother clinging to Adam. "I know about them, Ella." Dicky Harmond swirled by. He held his leg as if it pained him. "That is where the pills came from, isn't Ella?" She was slowly getting the pieces. "But who gave Father the pills? How did they disguise it?" Her father's body appeared. Shandra gasped and started crying.

Ryan had hesitated to wake Shandra when she'd whimpered. If her grandmother was showing Shandra clues, he didn't want to wake her up. But her tears and sniffles, he couldn't ignore.

He reached across and grasped Shandra's shoulder, giving her a gentle shake. "Shandra? Shandra, honey. Wake up." They were only twenty minutes from turning down her drive. He didn't want Lil to think he'd made Shandra cry.

"Come on, wake up." He gave her shoulder another little shake.

"Take me out of here, Ella. I don't want to see him like this." Shandra's plea sounded like a small child's.

Ryan pulled the Jeep onto the shoulder of the road, parked, and pulled Shandra into his arms. "Wake up, Shandra. It's a dream. All a dream. Come on, honey. Wake up and talk to me."

Shandra's head moved back and forth as if she were trying to shake the dream from her mind.

"That's it. Come on. Tell me about it." Ryan pushed her long strands of dark hair out of her face.

Her eye lashes fluttered and her lids opened, giving him a close-up view of her golden eyes. They reminded him of a topaz stone he saw in a jewelry store in Chicago.

She stiffened in his arms.

"It's okay. I've got you." He brushed a thumb across her cheek, wiping away tears.

"Why are we stopped?" she asked.

"Because you sounded so sad and were crying. I wanted to wake you up." He allowed her to move out of his arms and sit up in her seat.

"It was a dream with Ella. She showed me Mother and Adam." The scorn in her tone, told him what she'd seen. "Then Dicky Harmond, holding his knee as if he were in pain. I think it's a clue to where the painkillers came from. But if he gave them to Father, and Phil was pretty certain Father would never take anything from Dicky, then someone connected to Dicky had to have slipped them to Father."

"Was there anyone else in the dream?" Ryan

wondered that any of that would have made her cry like a child.

She gulped and stared out the front windshield. "Only my father's battered body." She wiped at tears that had slipped out of her eyes and down her cheeks. "Why does she keep showing me Father all torn up and bloody?" Shandra peered at him with such sorrow his heart ached.

Chapter Twenty-eight

Shandra took a long hot shower and was dressed in her favorite pajamas, but she was reluctant to go to bed. The dream she'd had while sleeping in the Jeep, didn't bode well for what she might encounter should she lay down on her bed.

Ryan sat on the couch, his computer on his lap, and a beer on the table in front of him.

"Mind if I join you?" she asked, motioning to the couch beside him.

He smiled. "I never turn down a chance to sit next to you." He clicked some keys and started to put the computer on the table.

"No, you don't have to stop what you're doing. I just don't feel like closing my eyes."

Sheba rose from her spot in front of the fireplace and lumbered over to the couch, placing her basketball-size head on Shandra's lap.

"Do you need to go out?" Shandra asked.

Sheba woofed and trotted toward the kitchen and back door.

"I'll take care of it." Ryan rose and followed Sheba to the kitchen.

Shandra peeked at what Ryan was studying on his computer. It appeared to be arrest records. But whose?

Ryan's slippers slapped the wood floor as he returned to the room. "I'm glad Lil moved back to her room in the barn while we were gone today. I don't think my back could take another night on this couch."

"Yes. But I still worry about her out there with her cast. She could fall and injure something else swinging around on crutches." Shandra was also glad to have Lil out of the house. It was hard to feel comfortable around Ryan with Lil watching their every move.

"She's a tough old bird. She'll be fine." He placed his computer back on his lap.

"Whose arrest record are you looking up?" she asked.

He glanced at her. "Everyone who might have something to do with your father's death."

It took a minute for his words to sink in. "Everyone? Including Mother and Adam? They have arrest records?"

"No, but two people bailed Dicky out of jail numerous times. Before the 'accident' Jessie Preston bailed Dicky out twice for assault. After the 'accident' Walter Malcolm bailed Dicky out three times."

Shandra slid closer to Ryan and stared at the computer. "How did Dicky die?"

"A barroom fight." Ryan glanced at her. "What are you thinking?"

"If Walter didn't want Dicky blackmailing him anymore, having him die in a barroom brawl wouldn't have looked like murder." Shandra wondered if one of the people in her dream who was beat up hadn't been her father but Dicky. "How do we prove that Walter also had Father drugged?"

"You're leaping to conclusions. We don't know that Walter had Harmond killed, and we don't know that he pre-meditated your father's murder. Though he did make sure Edward rode a horse known to stomp its rider." Ryan ran a hand across the back of his neck.

Shandra had learned that tell-tale sign meant he was frustrated. "Here." She sat up on her knees and massaged his thick neck. It was the least she could do since it was her troubles that caused him tense muscles.

"Jessie said she wouldn't have anything to do with Dicky because he beat women. But she clearly had to have had some connection to him to bail him out of jail." Shandra leaned over Ryan's shoulder. "Can you dig into Jessie's background more?"

"I can, but it's hard to concentrate with you leaning over my shoulder." Ryan placed a hand behind her head and drew her down into a kiss.

It wasn't the first time they'd kissed, but it was the first time she felt more than pleasure. It was a connection of sorts. *I could have this every night if I gave in.* Before her body melted into his lap, she drew back. "I think it's time for me to go to bed. Good night."

He released her. The twinkle and heat in his eyes

said he'd felt her resistance falter. "Good night."

Shandra kept her feet from running as she headed to her bedroom sanctuary.

Sheba woofed.

"I'll get her!" Ryan called.

Five minutes later there was a knock and the door opened. Sheba bounded into the room, jumping into the middle of the bed.

Ryan stuck his head around the door. "I tried to get as many snow balls off her feet as I could."

"Thank you. She'll pull off any you missed with her teeth and eat them. That's why I have this waterproof blanket on the top of my bed." Shandra flipped the top blanket a bit.

"That's a good idea. Okay, well, good night, again." Ryan peered at her a moment.

"Good night, again." She wasn't ready to invite him into her bed. She cared for him, but was still hesitant after her last disastrous relationship.

His head disappeared and the door closed. Shandra drew in a deep cleansing breath and turned out the light.

***

Ryan returned to the great room and the couch where his computer had Jessie Preston-Lawyer's life blinking on the screen. His feelings for Shandra were strong enough he could stay out of her bed until she was ready to invite him. He knew something in her past had her shying away from her feelings toward him. But since he wasn't ready just yet to settle down, he was willing to wait her out.

Scanning the police records where Jessie lived, he noticed police were called to the hospital for a possible domestic case. Jessie's name was linked to Harmond's. He had beaten her up at one point. He cross-checked the dates she bailed him out. She'd bailed him out before he beat her up. But did she have a big enough bone to pick with Edward to give him the benzodiazepine? And how were they going to prove she did?

***

The next morning Ryan was up before Shandra. He made his coffee and put the tea kettle on to boil. He stuck his head in the fridge looking for ingredients to make an omelet.

"Good morning. You're up early," Shandra said.

He glanced over his shoulder. She was still in her PJs. Her hair was mussed, and he was glad he had cold air blowing on his body.

"Morning." Ryan continued digging in the fridge, pulling out eggs, cheese, ham, and broccoli. "Your water should be hot."

"Thanks." She made her tea and sat at the counter. "Did you discover anything more last night?"

"Yes. Harmond at one time put Jessie in the hospital. After that is when she stopped bailing him out of jail." He placed the ingredients on the counter next to the stove. With his back to Shandra, he said, "I called in and requested a couple days off. Starting tomorrow."

"It won't take that long to get a tree. Why would you need more days off?" Shandra asked.

"We'll get the tree this morning, then we're headed to Nespelem." He faced her. "We need to talk to Jessie. She is the only person I can think of who could have given your father the benzodiazepine, and then would have posed as your mom and told the police and coroner he was taking painkillers."

Shandra stared at him for a long time. He hoped she didn't think he was just trying to get in her family's good graces. He wanted to get to the truth for her sake.

"I'll need to call my aunt and make arrangements for us to stay at the ranch." She left the kitchen without another word.

Ryan continued making the omelets and wondered what was going through her mind.

Chapter Twenty-nine

Shandra sat in the passenger side of the Jeep as they raced down the interstate toward the Colville Reservation and possibly the end of her quest to find out who killed her father. Something in the back of her mind kept trying to come forward, but she couldn't quite get the information to appear.

"Do you have Jessie's address?" Shandra asked. "I don't know how early she goes to the Ketch Pen."

"I have the address." Ryan glanced over at her. "I'd feel better about this if Sergeant Quinn would call with the information about who hired that detective who followed us. If it's Jessie, we'd have more to lean on her with."

"Maybe by the time we get there, he'll call." Shandra sat up straight, willing Ryan's foot to press harder on the accelerator, so they would get there sooner. She had a sense of urgency and wasn't sure why.

They crossed the Grand Coulee Dam and soon buzzed by the Agency and the Community Center. She saw Aunt Jo's pickup in the parking lot. Aunt Jo said she had to work but would be home by four. It was three now.

"Are you familiar with the area?" Ryan asked.

"No. Not really. Let's try the Ketch Pen first. If she's not there, we can ask for directions to her house." Shandra gripped the arm rest on the door. Why do I feel like something bad is going to happen?

"Turn up here. There it is. That square building on the corner." The Ketch Pen sign made it obvious which building was the tavern.

Ryan parked and glanced over at her. "How do you want to do this? Both go in at the same time or you go in and if you don't come back out, I'll know she's in there and come in for back up?"

"I like going in separate. I think if two of us try to talk to her she won't cooperate." Shandra reached out to Ryan. He put his hand in hers. "I don't know what we'll find out, but I feel like time is of the essence."

"I'll give you five minutes then I'll come in."

Shandra nodded, released his hand, and stepped out of the Jeep. She wasn't sure Jessie would remember who she was, but the bartender and owner would remember her and know she'd upset his patron on her previous visit.

She walked up to the door, glanced over her shoulder at Ryan, and gave him a weak smile before entering the dark building. She decided this time she'd tell Jessie the truth and see what came of it.

As she'd predicted, the bartender took one look at her and started to bristle. Shandra held up a hand as she approached the bar. "I'm not here to cause trouble. My name is Shandra Higheagle, I'm Edward Higheagle's daughter. Is Jessie here?"

The bartender stared at her a moment then his features softened. "You were digging for answers about your father the last time you were here."

"Yes. This time I'm not playing games. I need to ask Jessie some questions about that day." Shandra hoped this man had a soft spot for her father.

"She won't be in until six. You can probably find her at her house."

"Where is that?"

"Go left three blocks and follow that road all the way out to the place with a red barn and arena with barrels in it. You can't miss it."

"Thank you." Shandra pivoted to the door, leaving the yeasty scent of beer, the stale grease, and unwashed bodies behind as she stepped out into the fresh air.

Ryan was just closing the door on the Jeep. He walked over to her. "I thought she was in there you took so long."

"No. The bartender gave me directions to her place." Shandra opened her door and climbed in. She gave the directions to Ryan, and before long, the red barn and arena came into view.

"There it is." She pointed to the drive leading down to a small, faded green house. It didn't appear too run down, but the house could use some paint and there were brown piles of weeds in the area between the house, arena, and barn.

The lights were on in the house.

Shandra stepped out of the vehicle before Ryan had the engine turned off.

"Whoa," he said, grasping her arm, keeping her from striding up to the door. "Take a deep breath and don't go accusing this woman of anything. Tell her who you are and slowly see if you can get her to talk about your father and his last day."

Shandra nodded as her heart beat faster. Jessie had to want to unburden herself after all this time.

They walked up to the door and Ryan knocked.

"Just a minute!" Jessie called out.

Shandra scanned the area, wondering where Jessie's husband was. Maybe in the house as well.

The door opened. Jessie appeared along with the nostril-burning, secondhand smoke that seeped out onto the porch. Her hair was in the style Shandra saw at the Ketch Pen. In the light from the house, she discovered the color was blonde with gray.

"What do you want? I don't give to churches or charities," Jessie said.

Good. She doesn't recognize me from before. Shandra held out her hand. "Mrs. Lawyer, I'm Shandra Higheagle, I believe you knew my father, Edward Higheagle, and my mother, Celeste."

Jessie barely touched Shandra's extended fingers and backed into the house. Shandra followed from the pressure on her back by Ryan, moving her into the warmth and light.

"What do you want with me? Just because I know them doesn't mean I can help you with anything."

Jessie backed to a chair and sat down.

"I've been curious about my father's death."
Shandra stared into the women's eyes. "I don't believe
it was an accident."

Jessie inhaled air, coughed, and grabbed for a pack
of cigarettes on the table. "Why don't you believe it
was an accident? That's what the police said."

Ryan's phone beeped. He glanced at it and tapped
Shandra on the shoulder. "Be right back."

She watched him walk over to the door and start
reading.

Jessie had lit a cigarette and started puffing. Her
fingers shook.

"I've discovered that it was manipulated for my
father to ride Loco that day. A horse that would have
never bucked my father off had it been a normal ride.
But nothing about that day was normal. I was left with
my aunt. Extra people were in the room when the riders
and horses were drawn. Someone gave my father
painkillers. Something he didn't need. Someone—"

"A blonde calling herself Celeste Higheagle told
the corner that her husband was on painkillers for a fall
he'd taken the previous weekend," Ryan interrupted. "I
just read the coroner's report, Mrs. Lawyer. Celeste
Higheagle doesn't have blonde hair. I'm guessing she
didn't back then either."

Jessie took a long draw on the cigarette. Slowly,
she exhaled. She was stalling. Shandra leaned forward
even though the smoke already made her eyes water.

"Jessie, why did you pretend to be my mother? I
know she was sleeping with Adam at the time my father
took his fall. You have never said anything nice about

her, why would you want to be her?"

Jessie's eyes filled with tears. "I did want to be her. I wanted to be Mrs. Edward Higheagle. Even if it was after he was dead."

Shandra patted the woman's shoulder. "I'm sorry my father didn't treat you well. Was that why you gave him the painkillers? So you could play his wife?"

Her head snapped up. "I didn't give him the painkillers."

"Then how did you know about it?" Ryan asked.

"Know about what?" Jessie asked, taking another drag on her cigarette.

"Know that someone had given him painkillers?" Shandra said.

"I didn't. Dicky told me this was my chance to play Mrs. Higheagle. That Celeste wasn't around and to tell the policeman that Edward was on painkillers from a fall." She shuddered. "When I said it wasn't right and how did he know the princess wasn't around, he said don't worry about her and do what he said or he'd break my leg and I wouldn't be able to ride in the finals." She squashed out the butt of the smoking cigarette and pulled out another one, lighting it. "That was my best year ever and first chance at Nationals. I wasn't about to mess that up. So I pretended to be Edward's wife and said what I was told to say."

Shandra didn't like the information. "Do you think my father would have taken anything Dicky gave him? A pill or food?"

"No way. They had a mutual hate for one another." Jessie nodded her head, supporting how sure she was of the fact.

237

"Who would have given my father something to eat or drink?" Shandra said out loud.

"The princess," Jessie said. "I saw her during the team roping hand him a burger."

"When was that, time wise, before the bareback riding?" Ryan asked.

"Team roping was right before the bareback riding, and Edward rode the last horse that day." Jessie puffed on her cigarette.

Shandra felt numb. Everything was pointing to her mother pre-meditating her husband's death. *My father.*

Chapter Thirty

"Thank you, Mrs. Lawyer." Ryan took hold of Shandra's arm, helping her stand, and leading her out to the Jeep.

"Breathe," he said, holding her in his arms.

She gasped and shook. "My mother killed my father," she said through clenched teeth.

"We don't know that yet. All we have are Jessie's memories about that day." Ryan opened the Jeep door and maneuvered her onto the seat. He hurried around to the driver's side and climbed in.

"How do I get to your aunt's ranch?" he asked, starting up the Jeep and driving away from the Lawyer Ranch.

"Go back to town. It's the only way I know to get there." Shandra's hands were clasped in her lap. She continued to look out the side window.

He had no clue what she was thinking. If he'd found out a parent that had treated him as if he didn't exist had killed his other parent, he would be cussing and trying to figure out how he'd missed it all these years. He glanced over at Shandra.

She wiped a hand across her eyes.

Damn! He wished he knew what to say or do. The highway was in front of them. "Which way do I go?"

"Right."

He drove three miles, and she told him to turn right again.

"Follow this for five miles." She continued to stare out the window.

"You want to talk about this?" he asked, wanting to help.

"No. I want to visit with Aunt Jo. Maybe she can help me understand."

"Okay. But I'm here if you want to talk." He brushed a hand down her arm.

"I know."

He traveled down the gravel road, peering into the darkness, watching for wildlife that could bolt into the road.

Lights blinked in the distance. "Turn left at the next road," Shandra said.

He spotted the road and turned, another mile they pulled up to a large, two-story, farm house with a barn and corrals to the right.

"Park beside the pickup on the left. That's Coop's," Shandra said.

Ryan parked. Three dogs ran from the back of the

house, barking. The light by the back door flashed on, casting light to the first pickup.

"Don't worry, the dogs are all bark." Shandra opened the door and stepped out. The dogs ran to her. She said something to them and they all sat.

Ryan turned the Jeep off and grabbed their bags out of the back seat.

Shandra waited for him to join her. The dogs started sniffing the Jeep.

"Come on. Aunt Jo is anxious to meet you." Shandra looped her arm through his and led him to the back door.

"Come in. It's cold out there," said a woman not quite as tall as Shandra but with the same facial features.

Shandra walked in and Ryan followed.

Three men stood in the kitchen. One had to be the uncle and the other two the cousins. The woman's smile stretched from ear to ear as she stood beside the man.

"Aunt Jo, Uncle Martin, Coop, and Andy," Shandra motioned to each person as she said their names, "This is Weippe County Detective, Ryan Greer."

Ryan held out his hand to the uncle first, then the aunt, and each cousin. "Pleased to meet all of you," he said.

"We are very pleased to meet you," Aunt Jo said.

"Aunt Jo, don't go match-making. We're friends." Shandra looked into his eyes then back at her aunt. "Good friends."

"I think that's a good thing. You need a man in your life," Aunt Jo said. "Andy, take their bags upstairs. Shandra in Coop's room and Ryan in your room."

"I don't want to put anyone out—" Ryan started.

"You aren't. Coop and Andy are staying with friends tonight. They just wanted to meet you," Aunt Jo said.

"Yep." Coop walked up to Shandra. "If I run into Jessie, you want me to let you know?"

Shandra shook her head. The last thing she wanted was Coop talking to the woman. "No. We just came from her ranch. You don't need to talk to her."

Disappointment shadowed his face.

"We don't need any more information from her," Ryan said. He rubbed his hands together. "Something sure smells good."

Shandra could have kissed him for changing the subject.

***

After dinner, Coop and Andy roared off in Coop's pickup, Ryan and Uncle Martin went in the living room to watch football, and Shandra stood at the sink helping Aunt Jo with dishes.

"What's on your mind?" Aunt Jo asked.

"How did my father and mother get along?" Shandra wanted to know if her mother's hatred of her father was sudden or smoldered for four years.

"At first, they seemed like all newlyweds. Stayed to themselves until you were born. Then Edward headed back out on the rodeo circuit, and no matter how hard he tried to make Celeste stay home with you, she'd pack you up and haul you around to all the rodeos with him." Aunt Jo pulled her hands out of the soapy water and faced Shandra. "To be honest, I don't know why they stayed married. You were the only thing they had in common."

Shandra ignored the burning behind her eyes. "I have reason to believe my mother gave father the painkillers that made him unable to ride Loco."

Aunt Jo wrapped her arms around Shandra and held her tight. When Shandra felt she could hold herself together, she drew away from Aunt Jo. "Ryan and I will confront her tomorrow. But all we have is Jessie seeing her give father a hamburger, Mother being with Adam at the time of the accident, and then hiding out at her parents' house until marrying Adam." Shandra felt stronger lining up what they did know.

"Your father and you deserve closure," Aunt Jo said.

"I know." She peered into her aunt's eyes. "The sad part is, I can see Mother doing it to get what she wanted—Adam."

***

The next day Shandra said good-bye to Aunt Jo and Uncle Martin at dawn. The plan was to make a stop in Warner to allow Ryan to get more clothing and check in with Cathleen about more information he'd asked her to gather. After that they'd stop at Shandra's to check in with Lil and make sure she was making out okay. Then, without calling, they planned to drive to the Malcolm Ranch and confront her mother.

Ryan's phone rang as they entered Warner.

"Greer," Ryan answered. He immediately pulled the Jeep over and hit speaker on his phone.

"Go ahead, Sgt. Quinn," he said, holding the phone between them.

Shandra clasped her hands together hoping this was

information that would help them.

"We couldn't get the P.I. to give up his client, but we had someone go through his phone. And a couple of the numbers made me curious."

"How so?" Ryan asked.

"They were from Montana. Both phones registered to the same account. M Ranch."

Even though she knew deep down her mother had killed her father, hearing the police gather information that confirmed it, stabbed her heart.

"Can you text me the days and times of the calls?" Ryan asked.

"I can. This M Ranch is—"

"We know who owns the M Ranch," Ryan cut in. "Thank you for confirming our suspicions."

Ryan cut the call off and turned to her. "Are you okay?"

"My mother and stepfather, people who have watched me grow, sent a private investigator to follow me." Her heart started racing. "Do you think they said to harm me?" They had both been cold during her childhood, but could they have wanted her dead?

Ryan leaned over and hugged her. "I think they had us followed to see how much we were learning."

"We know it all, now," she said, pressing her cheek against his shoulder.

"We do. Come on. I'll stop and get more clothes, we'll go to your house to check on Lil and get all our facts lined out." He released her and peered into her eyes. "It wouldn't hurt to get everything we've learned mapped out and confront your mother tomorrow. We're both tired today and need to gather all the facts before we accuse her, or your stepfather, of anything."

Shandra didn't mind putting off accusing her
mother of killing her father for a day. Once they went
over all the facts, she hoped to be able to look at it with
less emotion. Heaven knew, she'd learned to hide her
emotions well over the years.

"I like that idea." She settled into her seat, and
Ryan pulled the Jeep back onto the road.

While they were at Ryan's, Cathleen called. Ryan
hung up from talking to her and said, "Change of plans.
We're meeting Cathleen at the bake shop down the
block from the Sheriff's Office. She has hard copies of
all the info we've gathered. It will help to have it with
us when we confront your mom."

Shandra nodded. "When do we meet Cathleen?"

"In an hour. She'll come during her lunch break."
Ryan nodded to the door. "Come on. I need to do some
more Christmas shopping. We can hit a couple stores on
the way to the bakery."

Shandra shrugged. It would help keep her mind off
what was about to happen. She had her presents bought.
Chew toys for Sheba, catnip for Lewis, a new purple
scarf and slippers for Lil, and treats for the horses. She
glanced at Ryan. He might be at her house for
Christmas this year. *I should get a present for Ryan.*

They climbed into the Jeep and drove to downtown
Warner. Ryan parked and they walked hand in hand
along the street peering in shops until Ryan stopped at
one. "That would be perfect for my niece." His face lit
up at the mention of his niece.

From their conversations she knew he coveted
family. He had a wonderful family, one that loved him

245

unconditionally. And she… well, her family consisted of liars and murderers.

Ella came to mind. Not all her family, only the one side. Instead of dwelling on what she was about to lose, she needed to dwell on what she was gaining—A large family who loved her.

Chapter Thirty-one

The day was giving way to night by the time they drove up the drive to Shandra's place. Ryan had kept the conversation with Cathleen light and kept their shopping trip happy and carefree. All that they'd learned and was about to go down had to be weighing on Shandra.

The Christmas lights twinkled on the front of the house, studio, and barn. "I like the lights," Ryan said.

"I can't take any credit. Lil put them up." The awe in Shandra's voice said she underestimated the woman as much as he did.

"Well, she did a great job." Ryan stopped in front of the house. "We'll take the bags in, and I'll put the Jeep in the barn."

"I can take the bags." Shandra grabbed the handles on both bags and stepped out of the Jeep.

"Be in soon." Ryan drove the Jeep to the barn, opened the doors, and drove the vehicle to its usual spot.

He noted the light on under the door of Lil's room. It wouldn't hurt to get her up to speed on what was happening. Just in case this all hit Shandra after he was back at work.

Ryan knocked on the door. No answer. He lifted the latch and opened the door slowly, fearful of the barn door being open and the cat getting out again. "Lil?" He slipped in and discovered Lewis curled up on the bed and no Lil. "Is she in the house?" he asked the cat.

Lewis raised his head, winked, and closed both eyes, lowering his head back down.

"I'll take that as a, 'yes.'"

Ryan exited the room and headed to the barn door. The horses nickered. In the growing darkness, he couldn't see if they'd been fed or not. Lil would take care of it when she returned. He closed the barn doors and headed to the back door of the house. Three feet from the door, he wondered why Sheba hadn't greeted them.

***

Shandra entered the house with her backpack and Ryan's duffel. She dropped both on the floor, wondering why Sheba hadn't greeted her.

"Sheba!" she called. Whimpering and scratching came from her bedroom. Why would Lil lock Sheba in the bedroom? She started across the great room.

"Don't let that dog out," ordered a voice that had stopped her heart more times than she could count growing up.

She pivoted toward the voice. Standing in the shadowed corner was her stepfather.

"What are you doing here?" she asked, scanning him for any sign of a weapon.

"You never did invite us here after you purchased this place with money that should have went to your mother." Adam stepped out of the shadow, his hands in the pockets of his coat.

"Where's Lil?" Shandra asked, fearing for her friend.

"She's locked up as a crazy person should be." A lopsided smile flickered on Adam's chiseled features before the glint in his eyes took away all sense of mirth.

"If you hurt her…"

"You'll what? Turn me into your boyfriend?" Adam said the word as if it left a bad taste in his mouth.

"Why are you here?" She had a suspicion it was to make sure she didn't pry anymore. But how far would he go? He'd murdered once already.

"To make sure you stop hounding your mother about Edward's accident." He motioned for her to sit on the couch.

The last place she wanted to be was sitting. At least on her feet she could make a run for a door. And Ryan would be entering the house soon. She wanted to be able to help him if she could.

"We both know my father's death wasn't an accident." She wasn't going to let him think for one minute she believed that anymore.

"You are the only one who believes that. And another little accident will take care of that problem." Adam pulled several of her scarves out of his pocket.

"Sit in that chair," he pointed to a wooden-backed, dining room chair that was set close to the fireplace.

"What if I refuse?" She crossed her arms. Stalling would give time for Ryan to come to the house and see what was going on.

Adam took three steps toward her. Before she could raise an arm to ward off the blow, he struck her hard. Her knees buckled. He caught her and carried her over to the chair, placing her on the wooden seat.

"You don't know how many times I've wanted to do that to you when you'd give me that look," he said, tying her hands behind the chair back with a scarf and using the others to tie her legs to the chair legs.

The stars cleared and Shandra found her wits. "I'm surprised you worried about Mother getting angry with you. I would have thought since you both killed my father she wouldn't have cared if you abused me." The words came out as harsh and rash as she felt.

Adam grabbed her by the chin. "You were the one reminder I couldn't get rid of. Not without losing the one thing I wanted most." He shook his head. "I never understood why she didn't leave you with Edward's family. She'd planned to get an abortion when she found out her little spat with me caused her to become pregnant by an Indian." Adam spat the word Indian as if it had a vile taste. "Edward's busybody old mother put some notion in Celeste's head that she'd have nothing but bad luck if she aborted you."

Adam paced around her chair. "We belonged together. Celeste and I. Just because I was held up that night and Dicky had to go and rough her up, which she said was my fault for not being there, and Edward, the good little Indian boy, saved her, she slept with him out of gratitude and anger with me." He slammed his fist into the rock fireplace but didn't even wince. "I tried for four years to get her to divorce Edward. She didn't love him, she loved me. She came to the rodeos to be with me. But she always had you with her. I convinced her to leave you with your aunt the day of your father's accident. That I had a wonderful time planned for the two of us and you were getting to old to take a nap while we made love."

Shandra's insides recoiled knowing she'd been taking a nap as a child while her mother committed adultery with another man. It sickened her. But she held her tongue. Adam's wide wild eyes and pacing proved he was getting it all out.

"I talked my father into exchanging Loco for whatever horse he drew for Edward. My father complained all the time that it wasn't right, Edward seemed to always draw the best bucking horses." Adam stopped and stared at her. "When you started riding, I could see you had horse sense too." He shook his head. "Damned Indian blood. It wasn't hard to get Dicky, who hated your father, to crush up his pills and put them on a burger. I knew he wouldn't accept anything from Dicky or I, so I suggested your mother give it to Edward. A way to make amends for the afternoon we were going to spend together."

Shandra swirled the information around in her mind. Her mother was an innocent pawn in the whole thing. I jumped to the conclusion Mother had set him up. Shame rushed through her in a hot wave.

A click shook her loose from her thoughts.

Adam opened the glass front on the propane fireplace. He reached underneath and started filling the room with gas. "It's a shame this nice house has to be sacrificed for your death."

Ryan stepped into the room from the kitchen hallway. "Malcolm, put your hands in the air." He raised a revolver, aiming it at Adam.

Adam laughed. "I knew you had to be around here somewhere. This makes it easier." He ducked behind the couch.

Shandra tried not to breathe in the gas as she struggled with loosening her hands. Ryan ran over to her, he pocketed his gun, and started untying her hands.

"Ryan!" She saw Adam too late to warn Ryan.

Adam slammed a heavy piece for pottery over Ryan's head, knocking him to his knees.

She watched in horror as Adam ran toward the hallway. He would get away, and he'd kill them.

She heard something hit the floor and a grunt.

"I got him!" Lil called.

Ryan shoved to his feet. Blood trickled down the side of his head. He pulled out a knife and sliced through the scarves. "Sorry. Get the gas off and open the windows. I'll take care of Malcolm."

Shandra covered her mouth and nose with a scarf and turned off the gas, then she opened all the windows and the door in the living room.

Ryan shoved a cuffed Adam down the hallway toward her. Lil swung along on her crutches behind them a huge grin on her face.

"What happened?" Shandra asked, giving the woman a hug.

"Don't tell her yet. I want to hear too, but I need to call and get a car over here." Ryan started talking on his phone as the house grew colder and colder.

Shandra placed Lil on the couch with a blanket, went to her room and let Sheba out, who immediately ran over to Adam and growled. He must not have treated her too well when locking her in the bedroom.

Shandra pulled on a sweater and a sweatshirt and hurried to the kitchen to open more windows and heat up water in an electric hotpot. She didn't want to chance any flames until she was certain the gas was all out of the house. With a pot of tea and some cookies, she returned to the great room.

"Where's Adam?" she asked, seeing Ryan sitting in the chair next to the couch, scratching Sheba.

Ryan nodded to a chair in the corner she'd cleared out to put the Christmas tree she and Ryan planned to cut. Adam had one of the scarves in his mouth and one leg handcuffed to the chair leg. He scowled and had a nice bruise forming on his forehead.

"Tell us what happened?" Shandra said, handing Lil a cup of tea.

"That idjit locked me in the bathroom. That's a pretty simple lock. I had it picked within minutes of him locking me up, but thought it best to not let him know. I heard you come in and couldn't think of the best way to help. I move too slow with this cast and crutches. Then I heard this one," she pointed a thumb at Ryan, "come down the hall and figured I could come out." She shook her head. "I had the door open when I heard him bungle it. So I got on my knees in front of the doorway and got my crutch ready and when that one," she nodded to Adam, "came running up the hall, I stuck the crutch out and tripped him. Then I sat on his back."

Lil smiled a big smile showing off the couple of missing teeth she had.

Shandra hugged her, cautious of the cup of tea. "I'm glad you weren't harmed and could help."

Ryan frowned. "I didn't want to shoot him not knowing how long he'd had the gas releasing into the house. When he ducked behind the couch, I wanted to get you free to get out of here before I pursued him. Never expected him to come at me. I thought he'd just toss a match."

"I guess he wanted to make sure you couldn't get away either," Shandra said.

The shrill ring of a police car started Sheba howling.

Shandra laughed then sobered. It would be best if she called her mother and told her what had happened to her husband.

Chapter Thirty-two

Shandra placed the last plate on the table and stopped to stare at the Christmas tree. Her heart sang with happiness remembering traipsing out into the woods with Ryan, their snowball fight, and bringing in the tree. They'd drank wine and decorated the tree that night.

It was Christmas Eve. Ryan and her mother were coming for dinner and to open presents. And tomorrow, her heart raced, she'd agreed to have Christmas dinner with Ryan's family. It was a huge step in their relationship. Having her mother for dinner tonight was a huge step in their relationship.

The call she'd made after the deputies hauled Adam away and she, Ryan, and Lil gave their statements, had been the hardest call she'd ever had to make. And hoped she'd never have to do again. Since that night, she'd talked to her mother every day, making sure she was handling the stress and the M Ranch that was now her concern, since she and Adam didn't have any heirs and Adam didn't have any siblings.

Lil hobbled in from the kitchen. "This place looks festive. Even more than when Pappy and Grandma lived here."

"I'm glad you approve. Would you let my guests in as they arrive? I have a couple more things to tend to in the kitchen." Shandra headed for the kitchen.

"You do set a mean table," Lil said in response.

Shandra smiled. It had been a long time since she'd entertained, and never here. That it was Christmas Eve and she'd be surrounded by people she cared for made the event more special.

Sheba barked two separate times. That meant her guests had arrived. Shandra was pulling the roast out of the oven when Ryan walked in carrying a bottle of her favorite wine.

"Need some help?" he asked.

"Yes. You have perfect timing. Open that bottle and place it on the platter with the four wine glasses." She headed to the door. "And follow me."

Shandra carried a platter of finger foods they could eat with the wine while the roast rested. She stopped at the end of the hall and watched her mother pick up the photo of Shandra standing beside her father. It was one of the few photos of her father and her she'd found while doing all the research. She'd asked for a copy and had it framed.

Ryan nudged her from behind.

She stepped out into the great room. "Hello,

Mother."

"Where did you get this photo?" her mother asked.

"I found it." She wasn't going to add while finding evidence to put your husband in jail. Her mother had forgiven her. She had been genuinely upset to learn the man she loved had killed the father of her child.

Shandra sat on the couch with Ryan on one side and her mother on the other. Lil sat in the nearest chair.

Ryan handed out the wine glasses and raised his in a toast. "To discovering the truth and a wonderful Christmas."

About the Author

Award winning author Paty Jager ranches with her husband of thirty-six years. They've raised hay, hogs, cattle, kids, and grandkids. She enjoys riding horses, playing with her grandkids, judging 4-H contests and fairs, and outdoor activities. To learn more about her books and her life, visit her website.
http://www.patyjager.net

Mystery
Double Duplicity
Tarnished Remains
Deadly Aim
Murderous Secrets

Contemporary Action Adventure Romance
(Isabella Mumphrey Adventures)
Secrets of a Mayan Moon
Secrets of an Aztec Temple
Secrets of a Hopi Blue Star
Secrets of a Christmas Box

Windtree
Press

Thank you for purchasing this Windtree Press
publication. For other books of the heart, please visit
our website at www.windtreepress.com.

For questions or more information contact us at
info@windtreepress.com.

Windtree Press
www.windtreepress.com
4660 NE Belknap Court
Suite 101-O
Hillsboro, OR 97124

73521847R00145

Made in the USA
Columbia, SC
12 July 2017